Madison Hayes

MADE FOR
Two Men

ELLORA'S CAVE
ROMANTICA PUBLISHING

$\mathcal{W}$hat the critics are saying...

∾

2006 ECataRomance Reviewers' Choice Awards Nominee

5 Star Rating and Heat Level O "*Made for Two Men* is an exciting, energetic, and wonderfully written novel of other worldly suspense. It has drama, treachery, love and heated sexual encounters. What more could a reader ask for? [...] There is so much to explore. I enjoyed my time with *Made for Two Men* and have every intention of revisiting the tale. Also, I look forward to reading more of Ms. Hayes work." ~ *Just Erotic Romance Reviews*

4 Cups "The dynamics of the story are fabulous. [...] The plot flows smoothly and is easy to follow. I could not put the book down. [...] The sex scenes are fabulous and hotter than molten lava. Ms. Hayes has created an amazing futuristic world that really grabbed my attention. I recommend this book to anyone who enjoys male/male/female ménage á trois as I do. More books like this one please!" ~ *Coffee Time Romance Reviews*

Recommended Read "I re-read certain parts because they were so emotionally effective that I wanted to feel those moments again. [...] This book has the perfect balance of suspense plot and romance, a to-die-for bad-boy hero, it's intense, fast paced, with beautiful writing [...] The pacing was magical—I was lost in the story, the words held me captive."
~ *Jeanne Laws Recommended Reads*

An Ellora's Cave Romantica Publication

www.ellorascave.com

Made for Two Men

ISBN 9781419954283
ALL RIGHTS RESERVED.
Made For Two Men Copyright © 2006 Madison Hayes
Edited by Pamela Campbell.
Cover art by Syneca.

This book printed in the U.S.A. by Jasmine–Jade Enterprises, LLC.

Electronic book Publication January 2006
Trade paperback Publication January 2008

Also by Madison Hayes

ℬ

Alpha Romeos *with Rhyannon Byrd*
Dye's Kingdom: Wanting It Forever
Enter the Dragon (*anthology*)
His Female
His Mistress
In the Arms of Danger
Kingdom of Khal: Redeeming Davik
Kingdom of Yute: Tor's Betrayal
Made for Two Rivals
Miss February
Miss April
Miss August
Miss December
Miss March
Miss May
Miss October
Zeke's Hands

About the Author

ဢ

I slung the heavy battery pack around my hips and cinched it tight—or tried to.

"Damn." Brian grabbed an awl. Leaning over me, he forged a new hole in the loose belt looped around my waist.

"Any advice?" I asked him as I pulled the belt tight.

"Yeah. Don't reach for the ore cart until it starts moving, then jump on the back and immediately duck your head. The voltage in the overhead cable won't just kill you. It'll blow you apart."

That was my first day on my first job. Employed as an engineer, I've worked in an underground mine that went up—inside a mountain. I've swung over the Ohio River in a tiny cage suspended from a crane in the middle of an electrical storm. I've hung 30 feet in the air over the Hudson River at midnight in an aluminum boat—suspended from a floating barge at the height of a blizzard, while snowplows on the bridge overhead rained slush and salt down on my shoulders. You can't do this sort of work without developing a sense of humor, and a sense of adventure.

New to publishing, both my reading and writing habits are subject to mood and I usually have several stories going at once. When I need a really good idea for a story, I clean toilets. Now there's an activity that engenders escapism.

I was surveying when I met my husband. He was my 'rod man'. While I was trying to get my crosshairs on his stadia rod, he dropped his pants and mooned me. Next thing I know, I've got the backside of paradise in my viewfinder. So I grabbed the walkie-talkie. "That's real nice," I told him, "but would you please turn around? I'd rather see the other side."

…it was love at first sight.

Madison welcomes comments from readers. You can find her website and email address on her author bio page at www.ellorascave.com.

Tell Us What You Think

We appreciate hearing reader opinions about our books. You can email us at Comments@EllorasCave.com.

MADE FOR TWO MEN

જી

Dedication

&

For Robert O…

Chapter One

৯০

"I didn't think imps still walked the planet."

"What's that?" Danjer asked.

With a minute gesture, Saxon inclined his head. The tiny signal didn't go unnoticed. Ten years together had to be good for something. The two men had the act of communication stripped down to a precise minimum of words and actions. Particularly when the communication was important. Like when there was a life hanging in the balance, for instance. Or where there was a woman involved.

Danjer followed his friend's gaze up the busy road.

In a deluge of humanity, pedestrians swept inexorably past—though it was hard to overlook the huge eddy that had formed just upstream from where the men stood. The populace of Aranthea gave the two tall warriors a wide berth. Husbands guided their wives and families aside as they put some careful distance between themselves and the two fighting men. Gangs of youths stepped off the sidewalk to get out of their way while regarding the weapons they wore with keen interest. Women regarded their faces with almost the same expression.

As far as Danjer could tell, the northern town of Aranthea had emptied its entire contents out onto its streets. A low, wide dustro-harvester glided noiselessly past, cleaving its way through the ocean of pedestrians. These huge mobile factories moved between farm and city, processing and packaging as they traveled to market. This one was only noteworthy because it was in his way—obstructing his view—along with the crowds of eYonans who bustled along the iron-paved thoroughfare.

Still, neither the crowds nor the harvester stopped Danjer from identifying the object of Saxon's interest, making her way up the sidewalk on the opposite side of the road.

As he slouched beside his friend, his shoulder propping up the stone wall of a small shop, Danjer's gaze narrowed to focus on the long, slender legs that took the paved roadway at a businesslike pace, and with a decidedly sexy slant. Shifting his hips and tilting his head in an attempt to view the woman uninterrupted, Danjer followed those long legs up to their apex, lingering there an instant to appreciate the way her leggings wrapped her hips. From there, his avid gaze continued up over her jeweled bellybutton and her bared, narrow waist to finally reach a pair of jaunty breasts that swayed and bounced with each step. The sleeveless cotton shirt she wore was hardly long enough to cover her chest and *easily* short enough to be provocative. The buttons of her nipples were embossed on the shirt's soft, clingy surface, leaving very little to the imagination.

And Danjer had a great imagination.

Dragging his eyes from her breasts, he lifted his gaze up the long, delicate line of her neck to her face.

And there he stopped.

At the little pointed chin, the small pink kiss of a mouth — parted just enough to allow a glimpse of pearly white teeth. A light dusting of freckles brightened her high cheekbones and the ridge of her long, elegant nose. Her hair was a shower of pale sunshine that reached down just long enough to hug her neck in saucy wisps, while a fall of the same warm yellow lay like a curtain across one eye.

Green. Her eyes were green. Meadow green. Quiet, yet full of life.

Danjer shook his head. "That's not an imp."

"No?"

"Too tall," he said shortly without removing his gaze from the woman striding up the road in their direction.

Saxon tilted his head appraisingly. "She's tall," he admitted, "and she's...she's...what's that word?"

"Willowy," Danjer supplied.

"Willowy," Saxon agreed in an awed voice nothing short of sublime. "Bet she can bend herself right in half."

"And I bet you'd be willing to help her," Danjer muttered. "What makes you think she's an imp?"

"Her hair. It's so...light and...straight."

Danjer nodded, rubbing one finger into his hairline. "Did you get a look at her nubbins?"

"Her feelers? No. But I'd like to," Saxon delivered, lifting an eyebrow suggestively. "I think her hair must be covering them. I didn't miss her nipples though."

"I didn't think you had," Danjer murmured.

The men watched as the girl stopped at a fruit stall that was knocked up against one of the tall buildings crowded together along the whole length of the street. "You know what they say about imps," Danjer reminded his friend.

"What? Kiss an imp? That's just an old mothers' tale," Saxon scoffed in answer.

Danjer nodded absently, his eyes on the girl as he recited the rhyme in a low murmur. "*Kiss an imp on impulse, kiss an imp for life, kiss an imp and take to wife, give your love and lose your life.*" Danjer shrugged. "There's usually some thread of truth in the old mothers' tales."

Saxon nodded. "I think we should test its veracity," he announced decisively. "Dare me to kiss her."

"*What?*" Danjer let out a startled laugh.

"Dare me to kiss her. Bet me two gold," Saxon demanded.

The woman turned her face into the sunshine, tossing a tangerine in her hand, then sauntered up the street at a slower pace, peeling the fruit as she traveled.

"All right," said Danjer. "But if you die, I get your sword and handbow."

Saxon gave his friend a look of pitying impatience. "That's not the meaning of the verse, you backworld barbarian." He opened his mouth again and then stalled a few seconds as he appeared to formulate his explanation. "As I recall, the story was...that one kiss from an imp would rob a man's will for anything else. That the nectar on an imp's lips was so intoxicating, so...addictive, he'd never care for anyone or anything else in his lifetime, that he'd devote his life, his love, his soul to the imp—and would deny her nothing and live only to serve her pleasure."

"After just one kiss," Danjer put to him skeptically.

"After just one kiss," Saxon confirmed.

Danjer shrugged one shoulder. "It can't be true, then."

"Why not?"

"Because if it were, she'd be trailing at least a dozen men in her wake."

At this argument, Saxon's chin came up in surprise. "Perhaps she's never been kissed," he suggested.

Together they watched the young woman lift the tangerine to her mouth, watched her bite down on the succulent fruit, watched her wet lips pucker into a shiny pink kiss just before she swallowed.

"That's not possible," they both said in breathless unison.

As the men watched in rapt fascination, the imp glanced over her shoulder, using her free hand to provocatively brush off the curved cheeks of her dainty, rounded bottom. Provocatively, Danjer decided, since there was nothing whatsoever on her tush to brush away. Not a speck of dirt, nor even so much as a *trace* of lint.

"Oh that I were a glove on that hand that I might touch that fair cheek," Saxon murmured next.

Danjer snorted as he watched the imp.

"What is it about women that makes it so hard to keep your hands off 'em?" Saxon wondered aloud. "Take that one, for instance. I'll wager there isn't an ounce of fat on that girl anywhere. At the same time, I'm certain there isn't a place on her that isn't soft and…what's the word?"

"Smooth?"

"No."

"Silky?"

"No. No. More like crushable."

"Fragile," Danjer told him.

"Yes," he answered with a contented sigh. "They're so delicate. So fucking fragile. Like you could break them in two if you weren't careful. It makes you feel so…"

"Strong?"

"No."

"Powerful?"

"Powerful," Saxon agreed. "Like you could do anything. Like you could do…*anything*," he repeated with an absent smile. "Take that little slip of a thing." Saxon's eyes glowed. "A woman like that makes you feel like you could beat the shit out of anyone who'd dare to look at her the wrong way. She makes you feel like you could crush the man who threatened her and leave him for dead, with only the flick of your wrist." Saxon continued with a sly grin, "All because you know you could pin her to the ground with your weight alone as you shackled her wrists above her head and spread her legs with your knees. And there'd be nothing she could do about it as you pounded your cock into the tight little piece of paradise there between her legs."

Danjer made a face. "If you didn't mind the fact that you were forcing the woman, hurting her, making her hate you *and* ruining her for sex — all at the same time."

Saxon nodded philosophically. "Wouldn't want to do that."

"No," Danjer growled.

"Still," Saxon grinned. "It's nice to think about."

Danjer shook his head. "You're full of shit, Saxon."

Saxon lifted an eyebrow in question.

"As big as you are, I've never seen a man gentler with a woman."

"Yeah, I'm gentle," he laughed. "But I'm just waiting to find the woman who'll let me tie her down and fuck her till she screams."

"You've been hanging around me too long," Danjer muttered, flicking his gaze sideways.

"That goes without saying."

"But if she lets you tie her down, you won't be forcing her."

"Hey! It's my fantasy," Saxon argued with a cocky grin. "Don't ruin it."

Danjer snorted. "Like you could force a woman, Saxon."

Saxon shook his head. "I just...like the way a woman makes me feel," he tried to explain. "Powerful," he finished off in a word.

The woman slowed her gait as she neared them, halting when she was almost directly across the road. With the tangerine resting absently against one cheek, she tossed her head fractionally. For a single brief instant, Danjer caught a glimpse of one delicate peach-pale nubbin at the top of her forehead, peeking shyly from behind the veil of her hair. Her chin tipped downward as she lowered her eyes demurely. Her golden lashes swept her pale cheeks for an instant before she lifted her gaze and gave the two men the entirety of her shy, lascivious interest.

The green glow of her gaze shooting across the space of the road was almost enough to knock Danjer a step backward.

With battleground reflexes, the two men responded at once, each reaching out to grip his companion's arm, using that as leverage to propel himself forward at the same time he tried to put his friend behind him. Normally, this act was carried out with his friend's well-being in mind, usually on the battlefield. All for one, and all that.

But not this time.

This was more of an every-man-for-himself moment.

With a twist of her shapely hips, the slender imp turned and disappeared inside the doors of a street-side tavern.

"Did you see that?" Danjer breathed.

"She was pulling me," Saxon proclaimed.

"*You!* That look was for me, you great ignorant outlander!"

There was an instant's silence. "I'm thinking maybe it was for both of us," Saxon quickly compromised.

"Yeah, well I'm not thinking in terms of 'both of us', Saxon. I'm thinking more in terms of 'me and her'."

Danjer took a step toward the tavern, but Saxon halted him with a huge hand fisted in his leather collar. "Let's be reasonable, Danjer," he protested. "There's no reason we can't—"

"Forget it, Saxon. I'm not one to share."

"What about that time in Geveena? After the concert?"

"That was different."

"Why?"

"Because that was the whole band. And the girls were...groupies."

"What about that girl in Vezinea?"

"That— I was drunk," Danjer said. "I didn't know what I was doing," he added. "I disremember the whole occasion," he finished off as he wrestled to separate himself from Saxon's huge clamp of a fist.

Saxon's mouth dropped open. "You don't remember the innkeeper complaining about the noise?"

"No."

"You don't remember holding her on me as I took her in the chair?"

"No."

"You don't remember her screaming my name while you stretched her legs wide and I fucked her with—"

"She was screaming *my* name," Danjer interrupted through gritted teeth, "and it was *me* in the chair."

Saxon's eyebrow winged upward in challenge. "Thought you didn't remember."

"I remember the chair," Danjer grunted, yanking out of his friend's grip.

"But she was screaming *my* name," Saxon persisted.

"Only if your name is Danjer," he shot back over his shoulder as he finally jerked free of Saxon's grasp and headed toward the tavern's door.

Chapter Two

ಶಾ

The tavern door pushed open, leaving scant seconds for Imprianna to carry out her mission. "That will be them now," she said quickly, then backed away from the crowded table to melt against the shadowed walls.

A tiny amount of white light blinked down from the few neon tubes overhead that remained unbroken. From her vantage point against the wall, Imprianna watched the two men push into the crowded room, pausing to blink as their eyes adjusted to the dark interior.

With keen interest, she assessed the newcomers as their eyes swept the tavern's clientele, looking for *her*, she assumed. The blatant once-over she'd given the men seemed to have worked, luring them into the tavern behind her. She shrank against the wall as the beacon of the dark one's gaze persisted in its search, while the fair one shrugged and turned for the bar.

Their cleated boots scraped a hard, masculine sound on the stone floor as they sauntered toward the bar, causing several heads to turn. A shiver went down her spine at the strong, virile sound that announced the presence of two warriors. The cleated boots were standard issue for soldiers and mercenaries—men who killed for a living.

A serving girl at the far end of the bar adjusted her position slightly, taking a tiny step and tilting her head to get a better look at the two intimidatingly handsome men. She wasn't the only woman to react in this manner. Several of the tavern's female clientele twisted in their seats to get a better look at the newcomers.

As Imprianna watched, the two companions exchanged a few words on their way to the counter where they threw some coins at the barman. While they waited for their drinks, she took the opportunity to assure herself she'd made a good choice.

They were taller than most of the men in the bar, with bodies honed to a hard edge by what looked like years of fighting. Trim hips led to long, muscled legs, and black leathers wrapped what had to be thighs of steel before tucking into knee-high boots. Both men wore swords on their hips, as well as an assortment of purposeful hardware on their belts, including handbows and ammunition clips. Their short leather jackets were open and loose, exposing a long stretch of broad, sun-darkened skin above the light jersey wraps that crisscrossed low on their chests.

The fair one was the taller of the two, with sun-crinkled eyes that shone pale below the high ridge of his brow. His straight nose and jutting chin made him a classic god where features were concerned, his mouth wide and generous with either a smile or a laugh. A spark of light drew her eye to his crotch. She smiled at the showy diamond that flashed and twinkled at the base of his fly, the eye-catching cockstone meant to ensure that his considerable merits would not go unnoticed.

The dark one was...different.

In a face as dark as age-worn mahogany, his eyes were piercingly bright in contrast, cold and clear like a frigid arctic sun. It was a spare, lean face, the weathered skin stretched tight over high cheekbones and square chin. Unlike his companion's smooth jaw, his chin was darkened with what appeared to be a sprinkling of black sand. Although she couldn't guess what caused this strange phenomenon, the effect was more attractive than she would have thought possible. Straight lines bracketed the hard, weathered line of his mouth. Like moonlight on water, the thin neon glow from the tubes overhead shimmered on the surface of his black, glossy locks.

While his companion turned to his drink, seemingly content to give up the search, the dark one put his back against the bar and rested his elbows on the countertop as he continued to scan the dark room. Slouching at the counter with an air of bored negligence, the man somehow managed to emanate a pantherish confidence at the same time.

But all of that was about to change, as the men she'd talked to earlier stood and shoved their way through the scattered tables toward the unsuspecting outlanders. Imprianna regretted the conditions that had forced her to take these measures. But she needed guardians. Needed guardians now. Thus the test. The two warriors appeared likely candidates. But she had to be certain.

Imprianna frowned. Actually, if she were honest with herself, she'd have to admit that the two men appeared to be *more* than likely candidates—and not only on the battlefront. Men like that would have to be good in bed, she guessed, if for no other reason that their looks alone were enough to make a woman just about melt and ooze into a puddle of want—warm and soft and sticky with desire. One look at the men had set every self-lubricating function in her body into overdrive.

They made her moist. She shook her head. That was an understatement. They made her wet.

She rubbed her lips together as she gazed at them. Vaguely, she noted that her lips felt roughly twice their normal size, thick and pouty and full of tiny prickling blood cells that ached to be crushed and smashed into oblivion under the press of a hard male kiss. Again, she rubbed her lips together, which only increased the uncomfortably stirring sensation. She felt as though she was all lips—and in more than one location. Besides the lips of her mouth, she was increasingly aware of the long, warm lips between her legs where her pulse drummed thick and heavy in her pussy, reminding her that she was a female and informing her that the men etched on the backs of her retina were all male.

Taking a long, shuddery breath, Imprianna pressed her lips together again and stretched. Her spine, from her tailbone to the base of her skull, felt tense, as though it needed a good shaking out. As she arched instinctively, her bottom pushed against the wall at her back. She accepted the wall's presence as only slightly better than nothing. What she wanted behind her was a warm male body, cupped against her ass like two spoons copulating. With this thought, her nipples tightened. Impatiently, she reached up with one hand to palm first one areola then the other.

Yeah, Imprianna concluded. If the men passed the test she had set in motion, they'd definitely do just fine in all other respects.

It had been seven days since she'd escaped from the Silver Duke, leaving him unconscious in his bed. Honestly. What had the man expected her to do? Lie down and spread her legs for him without a whimper? He should have known better than to leave a heavy piece of sand art on his bedside table. The blunt, irregular piece of glass had several handy protrusions just made for her grasp. He was out on the first swing.

Since then, she'd been making her way northward, mostly at night, across the sand wastes and into the grasslands, avoiding the main routes and angling west, hugging the edge of the forest when she finally reached it. Behind her lay the Copper Palace. The baroness couldn't have been too pleased with the Silver Duke for allowing Imprianna's escape. Ahead lay the long road to Judipeao. It was still in the control of the Iron Duke, who was part of the Northern Alliance fighting against the baroness. Imprianna hoped that Au'Banner would offer her refuge at the Iron Palace.

Glancing at the door, Imprianna shifted from foot to foot, impatient to have her measure of the men.

Danjer ignored the local talent shoving their way toward him in a wedge of surly humanity. They looked like amateurs. Spearheaded by a large, bald, bear of a man, the group halted within breathing distance of him as the tavern hushed, everyone's interest centered on what looked to be a confrontation of some sort and, with any luck, a fight.

They smelled of lemonale laced with stronger stuff, which probably accounted for their courage. Briefly, he considered asking them to go breathe somewhere else. He still hadn't located that pretty little imp.

With his hand on the axe that hung from his belt, the bald ruffian glowered at him as Danjer slouched back against the bar, his elbows perched carelessly on the countertop. When the local bully spat at his feet, he finally narrowed his eyes on the man as instinct tightened the battle-ready line of his long body.

Without so much as turning, Saxon clamped a huge hand on his biceps. Applying a considerable amount of effort, Danjer resisted the urge to shake it off.

"I'm sorry," Danjer said, his voice slicing across the silent anticipation that filled the room. "But if you like my looks, I'll warn you now, I'm not one for men."

Again, the local tough spat at his boots.

Slowly, Danjer looked down at his boots then back up again. "Your sister won't appreciate that when these boots are between her legs tonight."

A rumble of quiet amusement rolled across the tavern as Saxon unwrapped the fingers that clamped Danjer's arm, turning to smile at the local ruffian. "Do you have a problem with my friend...or me?" He drew out the last two words slowly, almost languidly, making it clear that the two men came together and would stick together, and would most assuredly fight together.

"I have a problem with mercenaries," the bear of a man answered with a sneer. "I have a problem with any man who sells his sword and kills for gold."

"Mercen...you're mistaken, friend. We ride for the North," Saxon told him. "We serve the queen and fight for the Iron Duke. We're on our way to Judipeao now."

As if on cue, the door opened a few inches to let a young boy slip through. Unaware of the drama unfolding in the quiet saloon, the lad made his noisy, breathless way to the two men leaning against the bar. "Captain Danjer. A message for you, sir."

Danjer took the message from the boy and, in the following silence, the bully gasped in a breath of horror while his face turned the old gray of cold ashes. Whispered murmurs passed around the tavern, from table to table, as the tavern's occupants realized they shared company with the North's most accomplished—and most deadly—warriors.

The local tough sputtered as his squinty eyes widened and his hand jumped to distance itself from the axe on his belt. "Danjer of Earth," he gasped, garbling the three words in stunned shock, then turned his gaze on the man who stood at his side. "And Saxon the Outlander," he stated. "My...my apologies to both of you." His eyes narrowed in confusion, then anger, as they shot around to strafe the tavern's dark corners. "The girl. She said—"

"What girl?" Danjer interjected sharply.

"She told me you were mercenaries and fighting for the South."

"*What...girl?*" Danjer repeated, his eyes flashing around the tables.

"There she goes," Saxon murmured, nodding to his right, and Danjer found her, slipping quickly along the dark wall, edging her way toward the tavern door. Her head was down and her face was averted, but he saw the sweep of sun-pale hair as she hurried toward the exit—and escape. And almost made it, too. Except that, as she reached the door, it opened to a tall aristocrat who barred the way.

"Imagine finding you here," he sneered in a voice that rang cruel with satisfaction. In one swift move, he had her turned, her arms trussed behind her as he pulled hard on the thin cord that he'd twisted around her wrists.

Involuntarily, Danjer winced. He caught a glimpse of hopeless resignation in her wide-eyed gaze just before the man forced her head down. Danjer's eyes narrowed on the hand between her shoulder blades.

"What's he doing with our imp?" Saxon muttered at his side and Danjer nodded in response. Together they moved toward the girl.

"I wouldn't have guessed you had an imagination," she gritted through her teeth. "It certainly never came up before." Then she twisted and cried out as he yanked hard on the thin cord that cut into her wrists.

"I've another cord for your neck," he hissed at the girl. "*Imagine* yourself strung up and dangling from it as you dance in my lap." With a final vicious yank on her bonds he dragged her out of the tavern.

"Hold up an instant," Saxon called out as he and Danjer pushed through the doors and followed the pair into the street.

The elegantly garbed aristocrat spun about to glare at the two men, his velvet cape catching the air to flare in an arc. Danjer gave him a cool, assessing once-over, gauging the man with his eyes and cataloguing the hardware on his belt as he took in the dark, curling hair, manicured fingernails and expensive leather clothing right down to his thick plastic heels, where razor sharp discs dangled from silver spurs.

The man reeked of southern opulence and southern arrogance.

"What are your plans for the girl?" Saxon queried pleasantly.

"Rape, mutilation and torture," the man enunciated succinctly. "*Not* necessarily in that order."

"Sounds like a good plan," Saxon told him amiably. "In fact, it sounds a lot like our plan."

Beside him, Danjer nodded. "We've a score to settle with the girl."

The girl tossed her head of sun-washed hair. "Hey. If you guys want to fight over me," she grunted at the ground, "go ahead and knock yourselves out."

The man continued as though she hadn't spoken. "I don't have time to keep score," he sneered impatiently. "But if you'll take a look around, you'll see the odds are against you." With those words, he jerked one shoulder toward the middle of the street where ten heavily armed men straddled their silent magnabikes. Floating a foot off the iron-paved street, the bikes were blocking the busy thoroughfare.

Saxon's brows rose in interested speculation as he observed the battle-hardened warriors mounted only yards from where they stood. These men were significantly different from the men who'd accosted them inside the tavern. Branded on arm and face with the white slashes of numerous scars, the men wore their old wounds proudly, like proofs of manhood. "Rough trade," Saxon muttered from the side of his mouth.

Danjer inclined his chin fractionally as Saxon slid his gaze sideways. When their eyes connected, they shared the same decision in the narrow blink of time. Danjer glared at the humbled girl for a few instants before he took a step toward her. With a fist in the middle of her short cotton shirt he brought his face close to hers. "I'm not done with you," he told her harshly, then thrust her away. With that, he turned and strode off as Saxon hurried to catch him, his hard cleats clicking on the iron pavement.

"Garage," Danjer spat out as Saxon caught up to him.

"Is this the way?" Saxon queried tensely.

"Yes." Danjer told him.

"We're going to help her," Saxon stated.

"We're going to *get* her first," Danjer countered. "We'll see later about whether we're helping her or not."

"We're going to help her," Saxon insisted in a low growl. "She was an angel!"

"*So* was Lucifer!"

"What?"

"A major demon on my home planet," Danjer explained shortly, "not to mention a major pain in the ass." Turning a corner, they broke into a sprint, their cleats clattering on the road's hard surface as they raced for the garage.

Chapter Three

$\wp$

Among those who fought for the North, it was a well-known fact that Danjer of Earth was the best tracker on the planet of eYona. Descended from an ancient race of hunters originating on the distant planet Earth, it was said he could track a log floating down a river at midnight without a single star to light the trail.

Danjer did nothing to discourage this widely held opinion of his tracking ability. It was almost true. In truth, it wasn't easy to track a vehicle that floated a foot off the ground. A magnabike didn't leave much of a trail to follow.

While large vehicles stuck to the iron-paved thoroughfares, most eYonans traveled by magnabike. The bikes weren't limited to the few paved roads that connected major cities. There was enough magnetite in the planet's crust to allow them to travel off road — through the needle-strewn forests, across wide grassy meadows and over the shifting sand wastes — leaving very little evidence behind to mark their passage.

But Danjer was the best tracker on the face of the planet. Of this he was certain. And he knew it was this belief that sustained Saxon as he glided alongside his friend, his lips pressed together in stoic silence as Danjer led the way south.

The two men had been together since they were teenagers, when Danjer's parents had immigrated to eYona. His family was fortunate to have escaped Earth's crowded cities, teeming with unrest, but had arrived virtually penniless. Danjer's father soon signed a five-year contract of employment with an eYonan family — Saxon's family. Danjer's father worked in the armory, creating lightweight copies of ancient

Earther long swords that were highly prized for their balance as well as their beauty. Many noble Northmen wore one of his father's swords, as did he and Saxon.

Enrolled in the same classes at educollege, the two tall youths were naturally paired for weapons training. They worked together where differential computations and electrical exploitation were concerned, and both of them benefited from that alliance. Saxon was brilliant when it came to mathematics and Danjer never failed to ace a lab assignment, regardless of the subject. But when it came to women, the men were rivals rather than allies.

Yet, despite their tendency to compete for the affections of the opposite sex, there were several times one or the other had to cover for his friend when he had a young lady up against the wall behind the field house changing rooms. When war had broken out two years ago, they'd traveled east and signed on with the north to repel the usurping baroness.

"What is it that you see?" Saxon asked him as Danjer concentrated on tracking the kidnappers' trail across a meadow of leaning grass sprinkled with fluttering petals and spiked with threatening bristles.

"It's hard to explain," Danjer answered, intent on the trail. "Bruised stalks, blades of grass. The grass bends as the bikes pass over it. Although it springs back almost immediately, some of the individual stalks remain twisted and the reverse side of the grass is…different from the front side. It's…duller."

"How do you follow a trail over the sand wastes?" Saxon persisted. "Nothing grows in the black sands."

"Sand bugs," Danjer answered. "The electromagnetic field generated by our bikes draws the bugs to the surface."

"Bugs! *How do you see them*?"

"Good eyes," Danjer told him distractedly.

As the sun tracked across the brilliant blue sky, they shucked their leather jackets and stowed them in their saddlecases. The pleasant scent of desert floss and meadow torch followed them as they whisked through the tall grass. They followed the girl and her captors for the rest of the afternoon, carefully halting at every rise to make sure the men they trailed were still out of sight.

"How far ahead are they?" Saxon asked at one such stop, frowning with consternation as his friend slowed beside him.

"No more than a mile," Danjer reassured him.

"Just don't let us fall too far behind," Saxon advised.

A long, open stretch of grassy land followed. When they'd crossed it, they found themselves delaying in the long shadow of a rock outcropping. The party they were tracking hovered astride their bikes, just visible at the edge of another wide meadow.

Tucked behind the tall prow of dark sandstone, the two men waited for the imp's abductors to continue into the forest that bordered the open field. As dusk began to darken their surroundings, they watched the group collect at the forest's edge. From out of the east, distant thunder preceded the inevitable evening storm as Danjer eyed the dark clouds forming over the plains. Shifting impatiently in his saddle, he squinted across the open field. "We'll wait until they move on," he instructed Saxon.

But moments later Danjer cursed quietly as he realized their quarry was making camp just inside the trees, with the long open meadow standing between them. The air thickened with tense expectancy as the electrical storm approached. The tall meadow growth rustled with static impatience. Silently, he considered their options. In an hour, the dark storm clouds would combine with falling night to cover their advance. Until then, their approach would be detected as they moved across the long expanse of open land. It would be best to wait. "It'll be dark soon," he told Saxon.

Saxon considered this statement. "But it might not be soon enough," he said quietly.

Blowing out a sigh, Danjer nodded. Saxon was right. They couldn't risk the wait. Not if they wanted to stop the ugly aristocrat before he carried out the threats he'd detailed earlier. Danjer hadn't much cared for those details and he expected the imp would like them even less.

"So much for a surprise attack," he grunted, swinging his bike around and engaging the electromagnetic drive with a rap of his fist. With a deep laugh, Saxon threw a switch on his bike's console as the vehicle surged forward. The wind slashed at their faces as they raced hell-bent-for-leather across the open field. Beside him, Saxon's hair streamed out behind him like a tangled gold banner. Long meadow grass flecked with bits of flowery color parted before them as they raced across the open field, bouncing over groundwood trunks and leaving in their wake two narrow ribbons of flattened grass. An ocean of rustling green rushed in on either side of their narrow track as the grass bounced and swished, obscuring their trail.

As it turned out, their opponents *were* surprised.

As the aristocrat's men rushed to seize their weapons and face the two warriors hurtling silently toward them, four of them were caught in the first volley as the two bikes diverged just before reaching the camp. Speeding along on either side of them, the four men were fried as the bikes exchanged a five hundred volt electrostatic charge. Like a blinding, crackling scythe of white-hot fire, it cut through the men, leaving them dead and smoldering before they'd hit the ground.

Danjer's sword came out, ripping through the air as he accelerated past a fifth man, separating his head from his body. Wheeling his bike sharply, Danjer jumped from his saddle to land on his feet behind a sixth opponent. Tapping him on the shoulder, Danjer's fist, still wrapped around the hilt of his sword, shot forward to crush the man's jaw as he turned. Spinning wildly, Danjer immediately took in the fact that two men were lying dead or senseless at Saxon's feet while two more ran for their bikes.

That left the bastard on the bike beneath the tree.

He had the imp—stripped naked and hanging from the tree—straddling his legs as he sat his bike.

Barely breathing and barely conscious, the lovely naked imp hung by her delicate neck from a rope looped over a thick branch overhead. Everything had happened so fast that her slim legs still drooped on either side of the aristocrat's leather-clad thighs. His dick jutted from the dark hair in his groin—a fleshy spike—poised and hard and ready to use. He'd been preparing to pull the hanging girl down onto his penis. Now he struggled to push the girl out of his way, trying to reach the starter on his bike's console.

What occurred next happened more rapidly than anything up to that point. Danjer had the aristocrat by the throat, his large hand gripping the beast's neck, dragging him from his bike—punching him into the tree from which the girl was strung.

At the same time, Saxon scooped the girl into his arms and took her weight, slipping his hands beneath the rope that cordoned her neck like a cruel, sadistic necklace. Easing the noose open to lie loosely on her shoulders, he fumbled at the harsh twist that bound her wrists against her back. Then, gently, Saxon cradled the girl into his chest, checking her pulse, rubbing her wrists as he watched his friend for several moments.

"That's enough," he said finally. "That's enough, Danjer. He's dead."

Danjer stopped in mid-punch, startled by the sound of his friend's voice, having lost himself completely in the blinding heat of his fury. Saxon's voice reached him as if from an incredible distance—cool and strong in the middle of his own volcanic rage. Danjer stopped banging the limp body against the tree's trunk, blinking his eyes, glaring at the broken man still clutched in his doubled fist. With a final obscene curse, he thrust the body at the ground and turned to the girl.

By that time, Saxon was lowering the fainting girl to her feet, helping her to stand. "Steady," he told her kindly.

Together they removed the rope from her neck. Danjer lifted it away from her face as Saxon pulled it up, over her head. Then Danjer's hands were on the fine, delicate surface of her skin. He frowned as he smoothed his thumbs down the long stretch of her purpled neck, moving his fingers over her shoulders and down her arms as he checked her nude body for additional signs of harm.

Caught between the two warriors, Imprianna trembled on faint legs. The one named Saxon was behind her. His rough, calloused hands were on her waist and hips, running over her curves. The dark one, Danjer, stood before her as his hands explored her body with meticulous care. Lifting her chin, she searched his dark face. Smoldering anger lingered in his arctic gaze.

Out of the stewpot, into the fire.

He had a right to be angry—after she'd set a dozen men against them at the tavern. He was an Earther, and Earthers were known to be a volatile, passionate breed. Yet, despite his promise of retribution and despite the violence with which he had finished the Silver Duke, all she felt in his touch was tender concern. Even though Danjer still glowered hotly as his eyes skimmed her body, she felt safer than she had in the several days since she'd fled the duke's bedroom in the baroness's palace. Safe in the strong grasp of rough, weatherworn, battle-hardened hands.

Sagging suddenly, she slumped forward and both men reacted to catch her. As her head fell forward onto Danjer's chest, his hands cased her midriff while Saxon's tightened on her waist. "Easy, girl," Danjer murmured. "Are you hurt?"

"I need your help," she told him just before everything went black.

Chapter Four

ஐ

When Imprianna woke, she was lying on her back and her nose was cold. Rubbing it into the palm of her hand, she lamented the fact that her longish nose extended too far away from her face for it to stay warm under any but the most tropical conditions.

She shared the men's bedding. They'd moved their mats together and she lay snugged up between the two men. Dressed in her rescued clothing, she lay beneath a thin, rough blanket. But the night had turned brisk.

Pulling the blanket up to warm the chilled tip of her nose, she breathed in the rich scent of its owner. Raw and masculine, the distinctively male smell wrapped her in a strong, reassuring embrace.

One of Saxon's thick forearms was snaked underneath her head, doubling as a hard pillow while his other arm lay heavily across her hips. Lying on his side, his eyes were closed, his face mere inches from hers, his humid breath a warm caress on her cheek. To her left Danjer lay on his back, his hands behind his head.

As she rolled onto her side to get a better look at the darkly handsome man, the action immediately revealed to her the extent of her injuries. She felt beaten and battered and utterly weary, as though she'd been dragged through a dustro-harvester backward. Torn from the soil, stripped of her essence, stuffed into a foil bag and discharged onto a flatbed to be rushed to market.

As she shifted onto her side, Saxon responded drowsily, wrapping himself around her more firmly, his big hand tugging at her hip, fitting her curving bottom into his groin.

Except for the presence of the large, hard cockstone decorating his leathers and poking her in the backside, Imprianna felt cozily surrounded, her ass cupped in the warm curve of his hips.

She didn't know where she was. The ground she lay on was soft beneath a crisp layer of pine needles, which suggested a forest setting. A distant gurgle and splash indicated a river nearby. She could see that they'd traveled from the forest's edge, where the others had stopped. Where the Silver Duke had tried to...hurt her.

Involuntarily, she shuddered.

"You're safe for now," Danjer murmured. "Try to sleep." He half-turned toward her. "I'll keep watch 'til dawn. Saxon took the earlier lookout. Go to sleep," he commanded quietly.

Achingly aware of every muscle in her body, she gazed at him, wanting nothing more than to heed his suggestion and surrender to sleep. Her eyelids felt like lead. The rest of her body was somewhere around the atomic weight of plutonium. Although her body cried out for rest, she was nonetheless reluctant to pass up what appeared to be a golden opportunity. Tucked into bed between the two capable warriors, she knew this was her chance to make the men her lovers and ensure their loyalty...as well as secure the protection which was, at this point in her existence, absolutely, unquestionably necessary. With these thoughts in mind, she snuggled her bottom into Saxon's crotch, though even this small movement caused her bruised body no small amount of discomfort.

Saxon's breathing lightened and she knew she'd woken him. With his hand still heavy on her hip, he shifted his hips a fraction and tentatively pressed his groin against her cheeks. Automatically, she pushed back, feeling for his cock with her pussy, repositioning the soft seam of her sex against the warm press of his vitally male equipment.

She heard Saxon draw in a small sharp breath of interest as his hand tightened on her hip. His cock pulsed against the tender flesh between her legs, stretching in lusty spurts as his shaft thickened and grew — warm and wide and throbbing against the soft, sensitive pout of her pussy. She allowed herself a small inward smile. Saxon was *easy*.

She had a feeling that his companion would be more of a challenge.

Nervously, she glanced at Danjer, whose eyes were open and gazing up at the night sky. She knew he listened carefully as he stared into the darkness, sifting the silence for any whisper of danger. A breeze riffed through the forest, carrying a hint of dampness, the product of an earlier light rain. Overhead, the dark sky was freckled with the spread of a million blinking stars as a distant storm washed the velvet backdrop with the occasional glow of pale flickering light.

Gritting her teeth with determination, Imprianna extended a cautious hand to glide across Danjer's leather-cased flanks, slipping her fingers over his belly and into his groin. His body stiffened beneath her touch and she continued to slide her hand farther and lower as she gave her derriere a small, warm wiggle against Saxon's cock. Lifting her bottom and bending a bit at the waist, she coaxed the thick line of his erection into place between the lips of her sex. At the same time, her fingertips reached and rode over the base of Danjer's bulging cock. From there, they inched up over the leather-clad ridge and curled around his shaft. She slid her hand up his length, surprised to find his cock stretched and stiff — by all appearances ready for action. Expelling a sigh of relief, she curled her hand more tightly around the width of his shaft.

That's when he manacled her hand in his.

"You're tired," he told her, moving her hand slowly back to her side.

Behind her, Saxon raised himself onto one elbow as the two men exchanged heated glances. "She's working both of us," Danjer informed his friend.

Without removing his gaze from Danjer, Saxon nodded hungrily. His hand slid between her thighs from behind as he pulled her knee up and lifted her leg to rest across Danjer's lower body.

"I'm on watch," Danjer reminded his friend, almost angrily. "The girl may have more enemies *and* it's tick season."

"This won't take long," Saxon argued quietly.

As Imprianna watched, Danjer glared at his friend. "Did you see her bruises?"

Saxon's gaze dropped to her neck while his hand stroked the length of her thigh to her knee, which was nestled warmly in Danjer's groin. His breathing was hurried, uneven. "What are you trying to tell me, Danjer?"

"That she's doing this...even though she's hurt. Even though she's exhausted. Even though she can hardly keep her eyes open. She doesn't want it. Not really. Not now, anyway."

Saxon brought his hand back to smooth over her rounded bottom. As he watched his hand make a few caressing passes, he formed his next question. "Why would she do that?"

Danjer turned on his side to rest his questioning gaze on the imp. "I don't know. She's after something," he stated flatly.

Caught in the headlights of Danjer's measuring gaze, Imprianna blinked at him as she felt her determination and resolve falter. He was on to her. Nervously, she licked her lips.

Danjer's voice softened as he smiled at her. "What are you after, sweetheart?"

Staring into his vibrant gaze, the warmth in his forgiving expression mesmerized her. For several moments Imprianna considered confessing her motives, risky though that might be. She *needed* these men.

Gently, he curled her fingers around his thumb and lifted the hand to his mouth, brushing her fingers across the rough-smooth silk of his lips. "What are you after, imp?"

When she didn't answer—when she didn't so much as draw a breath, but just stared at him wordlessly—he pulled her hand down to his groin and rubbed her curled fingers along the long line of his rigid cock. "What are you after, little one? You can't tell me you really want this. Not now. You can't tell me you want both Saxon and me on you, riding you, front and back. You're far too fragile...right now." When she made no answer, he flattened her hand over his cock and held it there as he flexed his hips and rubbed the thick mass of his erection into her hand. She gasped as she realized his size and he smiled at her kindly. "And Saxon's no smaller," he murmured.

Pulling her eyes from his piercing gaze, she pressed her lips together. "I want you," she insisted, attempting to sound both confident and worldly. "I think I could take you, both of you...with a little preparation."

Danjer looked skeptical and even a shade suspicious. "Preparation," he finally murmured quietly. "Exactly what kind of preparation did you have in mind?"

Imprianna hesitated. Her reaction was a mixture of a little shyness and a lot of guilty conscience.

Damn. These guys weren't making it easy.

When she didn't answer, Danjer reached for the top of her leggings. "Saxon," he said as he unbuttoned her pants, then let Saxon pull them down her legs and off her feet. After getting rid of her pants and shorts, Saxon stretched on his side behind her, pulling her legs open and lifting her knee onto his leather-clad thigh. She felt a cool rush of air as her labia parted, and Danjer's eyes drifted to the cloud of curls on her mound.

Beneath his burning gaze, her aches and pains faded. They were replaced by a much deeper ache as she watched Danjer's eyes focus on the parted lips of her pussy spread in darkness between her legs. As though of their own volition, her legs fell wider as her knee moved higher on Saxon's thigh.

"Careful," Danjer advised while Saxon returned a breathless laugh.

"That wasn't me," Saxon informed him. "That was her."

Danjer's eyebrows lifted and he glanced up at her face. "What are you after?" he murmured, his gaze holding her captive.

"I-I told you what I want," Imprianna stammered.

She watched as slowly, seductively, he sank two fingers between his curving lips then withdrew them, wet and shining with saliva. Keeping her eyes on his face, she gasped when she felt his touch at the top of her open sex, warm and wet, fingering her folds, running through the open ruts that led to her vulva. Halting just short of her opening, his fingers rode back through her sex to stroke over her clitoris.

"You're not very wet," he pointed out. Although these words were stated with cool efficiency, Danjer's brilliant irises were almost swallowed in the voracious black of his pupils. The man was barely breathing. "You're going to need more than a 'little' preparation before either of us can mount you."

At her back, Saxon rumbled out a low, needy sound while slowly, masterfully, Danjer played with her clit. His finger sliding through her folds taunted every nerve ending in her body, urging her to spread her legs, to press her thighs wide and invite his finger deeper. She closed her eyes and shook her head. "I'm not ready," she admitted, then opened her eyes again. "But I *do* want you. Your fingers feel good," she ventured carefully. "But your…mouth might be quicker."

"Ah," she heard him utter. "I understand."

His voice was low and warm. His Earther accent was softly foreign. It shushed like the splash of water slipping over rocks. The sliding syllables in his speech gave the man a predatory aura and brought to mind visions of a silently stalking panther.

His hands glided from her thighs to her knees as he pushed her legs wider and moved down her body. His mouth brushed against the inside of her leg, then closed on her flesh as he used his lips to nip gently at the skin of her inner thigh.

"Is this what you had in mind?" he asked her, his voice lust-thickened as he planted a line of kisses along the tightly stretched flesh. His mouth traveled toward her hungry, sensitive, swallowing sex. She lay spread beneath the heat of his mouth, parted and vulnerable, splayed open and aching for the first touch of his masculine lips, for the lash of his rough, probing tongue. His black hair gleamed in the starlit night and all she could see was the dark cascade of fine silk shining between her legs.

A heavy, urgent ache and burn—an overwhelming need for contact—settled between her legs as she waited in breathless anticipation. She twisted on Saxon's frame, panting softly, desperate for the gift of a man's touch in her unbearably hungry slot, eager for the stroke and slide of fingers or tongue playing with her clit, teasing the damp inner surface of her labia, rimming the sensitive flesh at the base of her vulva.

Her chest rose and fell in shallow waves as she withheld her answer—the answer that would bring her the kiss that her body now yearned for. As she hesitated, she could feel Danjer's breath hovering hot and humid between her legs as he fed it against her fragile, feminine folds, while Saxon held her open, spreading her sex beneath the promise of Danjer's curving, sensuous lips.

"Tell me what you want," she heard Danjer command.

His hair swept against her inner thigh and her sex clenched sharply then eased open with a surge of new interest. "I want both of you," she finally moaned.

Both men laughed—a low, wicked sound, full of lust.

"You want both of us," Danjer rumbled. "Licking your pussy? Fighting for your cunt with our tongues? Trying to tongue-fuck you at the same time? Jeezis Skies, Saxon. This girl's into some serious sexual fantasies."

Easing out from behind her, Saxon lowered her to the ground and rolled her onto her back. "I'm game," he breathed out roughly as his fingers slid beneath the hair on her forehead, gently exploring her hairline.

Danjer nodded at his friend. "I want to hear her ask for it," he said. "I still don't believe she wants it."

As he said those words, one of Saxon's thick fingers ran over the small, sensitive head of one of her feelers. The tiny, teat-like protuberance reacted to the brief contact and a tremor traveled her body in a crushing wave. As her body trembled with a shuddering vibration, she heard Saxon's lust-roughened laugh.

"I think she wants it," he told his friend.

When he carefully prodded the nubbin again, she spread her legs with a moan, planted her feet, and shamelessly lifted her pussy to Danjer's lips. She felt Saxon as he withdrew his hand from her nubbin and leaned over her, felt the light brush of his breath breezing through the puff of hair on her mound. But still she withheld the plea for the sexual act that would move her toward release—the kiss that would ensure her safety. Once the men had tasted her climaxing cunt, they'd be bound to her forever, and she'd have the guardians she needed.

"By the Princess," Saxon murmured, "she smells like paradise. I've never…known anything like it."

Danjer's lips brushed lightly against the hot, plump lips of her outer labia as he answered in a murmur. "She smells like sin…and nectar."

Then she felt them. Both at once. The tips of two tongues, the press of two wicked, open mouths sliding into her pussy, prodding toward her notch.

The moment they found her opening, she knew she'd come.

"No!" she screamed, pulling her legs together and wriggling in the space between Saxon's hip and the arm he had planted on the ground beside her. "No. Don't! Don't do it," she cried, pulling away from them and curling into herself.

Saxon's arms banded around her as he scooped her up, stroking her hair while he whispered assurances against her ear. "It's all right," he told her in a gentle murmur. "It's all right," he repeated.

Then she heard Danjer's voice again. "Spread her, Saxon."

With a moan, Imprianna burrowed more deeply against Saxon's chest and felt the thick muscles of his arms tighten around her protectively.

"Saxon," Danjer demanded.

"Leave it," Saxon told him. "Leave it for now, Danjer."

"Leave it? The girl owes us an explanation — several explanations — not to mention a fuck. You don't take a man that far and just drop him."

"Let the girl sleep. We can follow this up in the morning."

Danjer growled like an animal. "She might not be disposed to tell us anything in the morning," he pointed out.

"She'll tell us," Saxon stated. "She'll tell us, Danjer."

As Danjer looked on, Saxon held the imp until she stopped crying, cradling her in his arms, caressing her with the shielding sweep of his fingers.

"What was that?" Saxon asked her softly, after she pulled in a shaky yawn and put a few muffled words into his chest. Danjer arched an eyebrow in question as Saxon shrugged. "She's asleep."

"What did she say?" Danjer asked in a low voice.

"It sounded like…never kiss an imp."

Watching her face thoughtfully, Danjer reached out and brushed several pale strands of hair from her cheek while Saxon gathered the straight locks behind the shell of her ear. A long rough sigh came out of Saxon. "I'm as hard as a spike," he complained quietly.

Danjer nodded. "Keep watch for a minute while I pump myself out. Then you can take a turn."

Rolling up onto his feet, he took a few steps into the trees. Parting his fly, he eased his cock out of the top of the black jockstrap that cupped his sex. With a grimace, he stared down at the thick dark flesh in his fist. He'd been stiff even before she woke. He'd been hard just lying beside her, awake and imagining all the usual things that a man thinks of when a woman shares his bed.

All the usual things along with a few unusual.

For him anyhow.

Not so much unusual in action as unusual in emotion. There was something about the imp that really got him going.

Normally, his fantasies involved a lush, passion-bruised mouth wrapped around his dick, straining to take him as he sat with his knees spread and a woman's head between his legs. With one hand caging the back of her skull, he'd work her mouth over his cock—his hips rocking, feeding his cock between her lips and working his shaft down her throat.

But this time he'd been more obsessed with the idea of getting *his* mouth between the *imp*'s legs, spreading her thighs and pushing them over his shoulders as he manacled her legs in his arms and pinned her lower body to the ground. He could imagine the soft, moist heat of her pussy as he brushed his lips across her labia. She would smell like heaven and taste like sin. He'd wanted to sip at the wet folds of her sex—to savor her fully, to spend an hour between her legs, playing with her pussy, torturing her cunt as she made small, whimpering, female sounds of distress.

He'd wanted to wrap his lips around her clitoris and suck at the little pearl until it was a proud, hard knot under his tongue. He wanted to feel her cream for him. With his lips sucked up against the wet heat of her open slot, he wanted to enter her with his tongue and fuck her cunt as she twisted beneath him, banding his arms around her more tightly as she squirmed, forcing more pleasure on her. Forcing so much carnal pleasure between her legs that she'd scream and shout and beg him to let her come.

That was what he'd been imagining when she'd reached for him.

Then she'd touched him.

Her small hand, stroking out the length of his leather-clad shaft had almost robbed him of breath. The light touch of her fingers gliding across the top of his scrotum and wrapping around his cock had been an unexpected dream come true. He'd surged inside her hand as his dick expanded to fill every square inch of available skin. As her hand had sneaked up his length, he'd held his breath, waiting for her to reach the pulsing hood of his cock head. When her little hand tightened around the rim of his sensitive crown, he'd thought he was going to lose it—and almost had. At that point, he'd reached for her wrist and pulled her hand away.

But the light caress of her fingers was nothing compared to the scent of her pussy spread open beneath his mouth. The sweet, enticing fragrance resting between her legs had been everything he'd imagined and more. Sin and salvation. Torture at the gates of heaven. At that point, he had thought there was no turning back. Exhausted or not, the imp was going to get fucked. Too bad Saxon had gotten in the way.

Pushing out a sigh, he shook his head. Good thing Saxon had been there, he corrected himself. With a silent nod of self-reproof, he spat in his hands and rubbed them together. Casing his dick in one hand, his fist pistoned down its length. His eyes closed as he returned to imagining. It had been dark between her legs when Saxon had spread her open. The sweet, pink details of her sex had been hidden in the black shadows between her thighs.

But he had a good imagination.

Imagining the imp's parted sex pulled wide for his avaricious scrutiny, he pictured his cock pressing at her opening, stretching her pink slit wide as he crammed his dick all the way to the back of her cunt. Bracing his weight on his arms, he'd rise over her and watch her face as he slammed into her—pulled his hips and slammed again. With his eyes closed and this provoking image in his head, Danjer pumped his cock into orgasm.

A quiet snort of sound marked his climax as he levered his shaft downward to spill out onto the needle-strewn carpet at his feet. Opening his eyes with a jerk, he stared for several moments at his cum spattered on the forest floor. With a sigh, he tucked his dick inside his leathers as he turned back to his bedding, certain that Saxon must be burning from his root to his cock head.

But when he got back, Saxon had his leathers open. Lying behind the sleeping girl, he was pushing his thick rod through the cleft of her ass, riding through her crease with each surge of his hips. Danjer grinned when his friend suddenly stilled, his eyes closing in ecstasy as he spilled out onto the small of her back—while the imp snored on, serenely unaware of either Saxon or his ejaculation. Wrapping his thick fingers around his cock, the big blond levered it down to spurt at the imp's bare, rounded derriere then rubbed his shaft into the cum he'd pumped out onto her cheeks. Saxon groaned at the end of his release—the sound something less than complete satisfaction—as he frowned at his ejaculate puddled on her feminine little ass. He sighed. "Do you think she'll mind?" he put to Danjer with a wryly remorseful expression.

Danjer grinned. "Wipe her off. I'll never tell—and she'll never know."

"And if she does?"

Danjer shrugged. "She started it."

Danjer only hoped that he'd get a chance to finish it.

Chapter Five

❧

Danjer was up with the dawn, rattling through his saddlecases in a deliberate attempt to wake his two companions. When he finally roused them, a good many minutes went by before Saxon disengaged himself from the girl, all the while exhibiting a severe case of sticky fingers. His friend was obviously reluctant to leave his warm bed as well as the imp's warm body. Finally, the blond giant sat up and dug through the bedding for the imp's clothing. As the girl wriggled into her silky beige shorts, he watched in rapt fascination. He wore the same worshipful expression as she donned her leggings and soft suede boots.

And when she got to her feet, Saxon continued to gaze at her with an equally bad case of sticky eyes. Eventually, he pulled on his boots and rolled to his feet. Yawning as he pushed his hands back through his hair, he ambled across camp to Danjer's bike.

Pulling a wafer-thin camp stove from Danjer's saddlecase, Saxon set it on the ground and plugged it into the bike's electrical outlet. "Am I cooking or are you?"

"If you'll bring the water, I'll start the tea and stir the tanbouli," Danjer told him. "The river's that way."

Saxon pulled two flattened pots from the saddlecases and shook them out, smiling at the imp as he backed out of the camp.

"You have tanbouli?" the girl asked with wide-eyed interest.

"We travel in style," Danjer informed her with an easy grin.

"Can I help?" she offered as Saxon descended the path to the river and dropped out of sight.

Danjer shook his head. "I've got this down to an art. Make yourself comfortable. We'll want a full explanation from you during breakfast, including your reason for setting those men on us at that tavern back in Aranthea." Pulling a small bag out of his saddlecase, he measured out a scant teaspoon of tea concentrate and divided the dark crystals between two cups. "In addition, it might be handy to know your name and to find out if you're expecting any more attacks in the near future."

"Yes," she answered immediately.

Danjer lifted his gaze to question her, his eyes tripping a bit on the green glow she focused on him. Impatient with himself, he struggled to master his reaction to the girl.

"Yes, you can certainly expect more attacks," she continued, "before you can get rid of me."

For several seconds she gazed at him unflinchingly. Caught in the headlights of her unsettling gaze, he found her frankness captivating, but he didn't let it show.

"What's that on your face?" she asked him. "Is it…tattoo work?"

He laughed, glad for the question that interrupted the strange spell she cast over him. He rubbed his jaw. "It's a beard," he told her. "Hair. Earthers—Earther men—grow hair on their faces."

She tilted her head, her eyes fixed on his lips. "It's nice," she told him in a soft, husky murmur.

And just like that, he was caught again.

A quiet rustle turned her head and he watched as she followed Saxon's climb back into camp. Saxon came up the path balancing two pots brimming with water. The sun's early morning rays glanced off his cockstone and the jewel winked conspicuously as he crossed the camp. Unexpectedly, Danjer found himself clenching his teeth as he watched the imp's eyes drawn to his friend's crotch.

Dropping to one knee beside him, Saxon placed the pots on the thin, rectangular stove to heat.

"Your life is in danger, then," Danjer stated as he scooped tanbouli cereal out of a bag and sprinkled it over the water. He stretched out his legs and settled himself on the ground beside the stove.

The imp dropped her gaze to the forest floor and shook her head. "No," she answered with a wry twist on her lips. "Not at all. They want me alive. The Silver Duke was just angry with me and meant to hurt me. But he works...worked for the baroness. His orders were to bring me in alive. I'm quite useless to them dead."

Danjer frowned at her. "Useless to them?"

The girl nodded. "There aren't many pureblood imps left. Most of my people migrated to the Ockott Galaxy back in the thirties. That fact makes me valuable to the baroness."

Saxon laughed with a snort. "Why? Does the baroness have a collection?"

The girl shook her head again and a few strands of yellow hair tumbled across one eye. She tossed her head to flick it aside. "She only needs one." She paused to take a deep breath. "You've heard the old mothers' rhyme?" Neither man answered, but considered her curiously. "*Kiss an Imp*?"

Slowly, Saxon nodded.

"Well," she told them reluctantly, "it's true."

"What's true?" Danjer asked.

She shrugged. "Pretty much all of it. *Kiss an imp and lose your life*. Not that you'd die," she added hastily, "just that, after kissing me—after tasting me—you'd spend the rest of your life attending to my every whim, subject to my bidding. The baroness wants me so that she can...experiment with my fluids. She has a fully staffed sci-lab."

The young woman swallowed, the muscles of her throat working against her pale flesh, and continued. "The confrontation I arranged in the tavern was meant to test your abilities. I wanted to get your measure before I...bound you to me. I needed guardians, someone who could protect me until I could get an audience with the Iron Duke. I needed protection and, although I didn't have time to be choosey, you two appeared to be likely candidates."

Stunned, Danjer gave her a look of disgust. "You were going to *seduce* us and...bind us to you without our knowledge? Make us your slaves, virtually? Why didn't you just ask for our help?"

"Why should you risk your lives for a stranger?" she countered defensively, a vivid flush painting her cheeks. "I didn't have much time. And I had to be certain of your loyalty," she muttered. "I'm sorry!" She hung her head. Again, her shock of yellow hair sifted over her left eye before she pushed it behind her ear. "But there's more than my life at risk. The baroness plans to use my...fluids to create a chemical whereby she can control men...command armies, control her enemy's armies! And if she succeeds, she'll either wipe out your northern forces or enslave every one of your soldiers to her will...forever."

"She wants your saliva?" Saxon questioned with slow incredulity.

Both Danjer and the girl shook their heads at the big man. "Wrong set of lips," Danjer muttered to his friend.

"Oh." Saxon blinked. "*Oh*," he said suddenly. Then his expression brightened. "So her mouth isn't off-limits then?" The idea seemed to please him to no end and Danjer couldn't help but smile at him.

"And how do you know all this about the baroness's...*plans*?" Danjer continued.

"I was working at a recharge station, south of Copper City, when the baroness's party stopped in to power up. When she forced me to join her, I though I was just being pressed into service in the southern army. At first I thought she was looking for an electrical augmenteer." She laughed bitterly. "But she'd recognized me for an imp."

She took a deep breath before she continued. "I escaped from her in the middle of her experiments, before she was able to get what she wanted. They couldn't make me orgasm."

There were a few seconds of uneasy silence. "You weren't...hurt," Danjer stated, finding the idea unacceptable.

Her pretty face pulled into a painful knot. "Not exactly. Although it wasn't pleasant. They tried a lot of different...procedures on me in an attempt to make me come."

"You weren't raped," Danjer insisted with a growl.

She shook her head. "I wasn't...penetrated—at least, not by a man, if that's what you mean. They didn't want my fluids to be contaminated by anyone else's. I was stimulated with glass rods, rubber penises." She screwed up her face again and it was clear she was close to crying though she forced out a brittle little laugh. "Do you know how unpleasant that can be when you don't fancy the man...who's touching you?"

"Oh, sweetheart," Saxon breathed, moving toward her instinctively as Danjer fought the urge to do the same.

"And when you're prodded and poked all day long, you...get a bit sore."

As though he couldn't bear to see her unhappy, Saxon pulled her into his chest and wrapped his huge arms around her. Fixing his gaze on the pot, Danjer continued stirring the tanbouli, glancing up only once. But that one glance revealed the imp watching him with the same kind of expression that was clearly stamped upon his best friend's face. And Saxon's expression—as he gazed down on the imp's head—bordered on complete devotion.

He'd never seen Saxon look at a woman like that before.

With a scowl, Danjer turned his face. How fucking inconvenient was that! Saxon was in love with the woman he'd marked for himself. It wasn't every day he ran across a woman who could…do what she did to him. Saxon, on the other hand, had been in love before. Often. Briefly, Danjer wondered if he'd be able to wait out Saxon's infatuation. He slid a quick glance back in Saxon's direction. It didn't look like that might happen anytime soon.

"But they couldn't make you come," he pressed her, dragging his mind back to the subject at hand.

"It's not that easy…for me, because I'm an imp. The conditions have to be right."

Danjer sucked in his cheeks thoughtfully, chewing on the inside of his mouth as he watched her eyes widen on the hard kiss of his lips. "You could have come if you'd wanted to? To get them to stop?"

She averted her face. "I could have told them what would work," she said. "But I didn't want them to…to…"

"That was brave of you," Danjer mentioned quietly.

"Very brave," Saxon concurred.

The water boiled and Danjer poured the tea then took one of the cups to Saxon, who immediately offered it to the girl. "It's hot," Saxon warned her, a look of worship lighting his face as she cupped his hands and sipped from the thin metal cup.

"What's your name?" Danjer asked as he returned to his stirring.

"Imprianinka," she answered.

"Impri—what?" Saxon exclaimed.

She made a face. "I don't like it either," she told him wryly.

"No. No, it's a fine name," Saxon insisted at once. "It's just a bit…long."

"I usually go by Imprianna."

But Danjer could tell Saxon was still worried about the name. "You don't look like an Imprianinka," he suggested immediately.

"No?"

"No," Danjer insisted quietly as he shook out two bowls and filled them with the sweet, fragrant tanbouli. His eyes flicked to the jewel on her belly. "You look more like a Pink. Why don't we just shorten the name all the way to Pink?"

"Pink?" she questioned. "Is that an…Earth name?"

"Yes," he lied immediately. "It's an Earth name. A very good Earth name from a great family."

The imp looked so pleased that he couldn't help but return her shy smile with a warm one of his own. "So you escaped from the baroness before she could get any of your…fluids," he prompted.

She nodded, pulling away from Saxon. Lowering herself to the ground, she sat against a tree while Saxon returned to the stove and snagged both bowls of hot cereal. Dappled sunshine strained down through the trees to caress the imp with a shifting pattern of light and shadow. In that moment, she looked like she belonged to the quiet, shadowed forest—a pure fawn of nature lacking only a male to stand beside her.

Danjer shook himself. Settling back against his bike, he grabbed a spoon, feeding himself from the pot while Saxon delivered a bowl to the imp and lowered himself to crouch beside her.

"That's why they're still after me," she told them. "If the baroness had gotten even a small sample of my release, she could have re-created it in her labs…in quantity.

"The Silver Duke was responsible for collecting my release. In order to make sure the samples were uncontaminated, the baroness had several of her people watching us. But the duke was getting more aroused all the time and more frustrated as he tried but couldn't make me come. Sometimes he would leave the room suddenly while he was trying to stimulate me. Once he didn't bother leaving the room. The witnesses made him wash his hands after he'd pumped himself out.

"He was getting rougher with me all the time," she went on as Saxon growled beside her. "And he was getting aroused more easily. At the end of the second day, he had me smuggled into his room so he could finally satisfy himself on me." Her face wrinkled up in disgust. "In addition, he might have thought I'd finally orgasm once I had a man between my legs. I got away from him before he was able to force himself on me. I imagine the baroness punished him for my escape. I expect that's why he was so angry with me."

She shrugged with a small, wicked smile. "It probably didn't help that I left a huge knot on his head. There was a large piece of sand art on his bedside table."

Danjer and Saxon shared a frank smile, smug with satisfaction.

"How did you get out of the palace?" Danjer queried next.

For a moment she appeared to consider his question, searching his eyes for some kind of promise. Finally, she seemed to arrive at a decision. "Imps can go undetected when the conditions are right. In a dark room. In a dense forest. In tall grass," she explained.

Danjer considered her keenly while Saxon asked, "What do you mean?"

"I'll show you," Pink told them and, with those words, she closed her eyes.

As the men watched, her face and hair took on the aspect of the tree at her back—not that she looked like she was covered in bark, only that the muted shades of the tree's mottled bark were similar to the shifting pattern of light and dark on her face. Saxon's jaw dropped and she opened her eyes again, returning to normal. "Of course," she said with a light, teasing chime of laughter, "it's much more effective when I'm naked."

Immediately, Saxon looked interested. "Let's see then," he encouraged her with a jaunty grin.

She grinned back. "You just want to see me naked," she complained.

Saxon laughed as he winked at Danjer. "Not at all," he protested. "I'm just…"

"Curious," Danjer supplied without even thinking.

"No."

"Intrigued," Danjer suggested.

"Intrigued," Saxon agreed. "I'm absolutely intrigued!"

"You're absolutely intrigued with the notion of seeing her naked," Danjer put in.

Unabashed, Saxon nodded. He shot the imp a mischief-made smile as he scraped the bottom of his bowl and finished off his last spoonful of tanbouli.

The bright sound of the imp's laughter filled the small clearing as Saxon got to his feet and crossed the camp to gather up the pots. "If you'll just point me toward the river again, I'll wash these up," he told Danjer, then sauntered off in the direction Danjer indicated.

Chapter Six

ळ

Pink's laughter faded as she watched Saxon's back. Frowning, she turned her gaze on Danjer. "What's...wrong with him?"

"What do you mean?" he asked almost defensively.

"You know what I mean," she said softly.

"There's nothing wrong with him." Danjer's gaze was shuttered as he unplugged the stove then stood and tucked it back into his saddlecase. "He just...loses a few words sometimes."

As she watched Danjer's grim profile, Pink's heart went out to him. His defensive reaction was a clear indication of his love for Saxon. She wanted to cross the space that separated them and wrap her arms around him. With an overwhelming feeling of longing, she considered the straight, hard lines of his uncompromisingly masculine face. He wasn't as handsome as Saxon but there was something about his primitive male beauty that called out to every female cell in her body. Especially now, in this instance, watching him with his shields locked into place, knowing he was vulnerable where this topic was concerned.

"I'm not talking about that," she argued gently. "He didn't know his way back to the river."

"His...sense of direction is a bit off," Danjer grunted, closing the lid on his saddlecase.

"A bit?"

Turning on her suddenly, his eyes narrowed in anger. "In most ways, he's fine," he said in a voice like sleet. "He can think and reason and remember. He has no trouble with math, reading, writing—and his logic is flawless. In a battle, he's…like an extension of me, like my right arm."

"And you're his left?"

"That's right," Danger shot back.

"How long has he been like this?"

Danjer pushed a button on his bike's console and the machine lifted into the air. "Ever since he took a blow meant for me."

"Oh!" she said. Then as the information sank in, she said again, "*Oh*!"

"Yes. *Oh*," he mimicked her coldly. "The blow he took to the helm a year ago would have severed my collarbone and taken my arm off at the shoulder. It would have killed me. He's my best friend—*and* he saved my life. That should give you a fair idea of how I feel about him."

At this rebuke, her cheeks warmed with guilt. Evidently her attraction to Danjer, along with the covetous glances she'd been helpless to hide, hadn't exactly gone unmarked.

"But, just in case it still isn't clear," he continued, "let me spell it out for you. I'd do anything for him. And I'd do *without* anything…if I thought he wanted it." With these words, he gave her a meaningful stare then straddled his bike. His expression was uncompromising as he gazed at her.

She was silent a long moment.

"Can't…he be healed?"

"Maybe in time," Danjer growled at her. "The doctors say it will take time. He has some swelling in the frontal lobe. But he may recover in time."

"You said a year has passed since his injury. Have you seen any improvement since then?"

"No!" Danjer barked back at her. "Maybe! I don't know!" Dragging his hands back through his hair, he glared at her.

Turning away from the bright heat of his burning gaze, she headed across the camp.

"Where are you going?" he called after her.

"To check on Saxon," she tossed back.

Saxon, at least, liked her. Saxon didn't glower at her. Saxon didn't shout at her. And Saxon didn't make her feel like an ass over an attraction she could hardly be expected to control.

She found Saxon at the river, finishing up, shaking drops of water from the clean pots and bowls. As he watched her approach, his eyes shone with clear male interest, his mouth turning up into a sexy smile. "Couldn't stay away from me, eh?"

She nodded as she smiled back at him. "Danjer's packed up and ready to go."

"Feel like a quick dip?" he suggested, ignoring her summons as he shrugged off his leather jacket and pulled his wrap over his head. Standing before her, he gave her a sinfully wicked smile. Slowly, he pulled his pants open then let them drop along with his black silk jockstrap.

"Show-off," she teased him, trying hard not to stare at the long, thick length of his cock stretching before his heavy, low-slung scrotum.

The man was hung! It was a wonder he could walk with so much going on between his legs. In addition to his deliciously packaged testicles, his heavy penis was uncommonly wide at the root. Her vagina twinged at the idea of that massive diameter stretching the tender rim of her vulva.

Focusing on a bulging dark vein, she tracked its wending path down his impressive length to the fat plum-shaped head at the end of his shaft. His cock wasn't fully aroused but it wasn't exactly lolling about either. She wondered if a monster like that was *ever* relaxed.

Dragging her eyes from his groin, Pink focused on his legs. His huge thighs were wrapped tightly with long, tough straps of muscle. His torso appeared infinitely long without his clothing dividing his length in two and his bellybutton was a curling apostrophe on the skin that stretched over his very flat stomach. His abdomen was lovingly chiseled into six impressive packages and topped by the wide expanse of his broad pecs, broken only by his ellipse-shaped nipples. His massive shoulders bunched as he moved and his fair hair brushed the muscles that sloped upward to support the thick column of his neck.

All of it was packed together so tightly, he looked like he could squeeze a man to death with nothing more than an enthusiastic hug. Saxon was built! Saxon was built like a harvester, though she doubted she'd ever find one with quite his sex appeal.

He turned, giving her a nice view of his handsome, square buttocks as he waded into the river and the water rose around his muscular thighs. Diving into the middle of the river, he resurfaced facing her, flicking his wet hair out of his eyes as he shook his head. "Come on in," he shouted at her from the center of the river's sunlit channel. "You need a bath."

She cocked her head at him, questioningly.

"I won't tell you how I know," he laughed. "But believe me, I know. You need a bath," he insisted, pulling his finger and thumb down his wet nose.

A rustle behind her turned her head and she found Danjer standing at the top of the slope. Tall, beautiful, darkly handsome Danjer, framed by two tall evergreens, with the sun behind him, emblazoning his strong silhouette.

If Danjer was so set on seeing her with Saxon, she thought with a wry twist of her lips, who was she to argue? And if she played her cards right, she might *still* end up with both of them.

Quickly, she shucked her clothing and waded out toward Saxon. The fair giant now stood in waist-deep water, apparently enraptured, watching her breasts as she pushed through the water toward him.

"What do you think you're doing with my imp?" Danjer challenged him lightly as he sauntered down the trail toward the river.

"We're just going to get naked and slippery together," Saxon informed him as he moved to join her in the shallower water. "Maybe have sex. But that's all," Saxon called back, pulling Pink into his arms. "And she's not your imp," he argued. "She's our imp. Come on in!"

As Pink smiled at Danjer, he gave the pair of them a semi-dark look. When he reached the riverbank, he ambled along the sandy bank to a fallen tree. There he sat. "I'll keep watch for ticks," he growled, reaching into his groin and resetting his equipment, then spreading his legs as he tilted his face toward the sun.

"Take a break," Saxon insisted. "Tell him, Pink."

This was her cue.

Pink gave him her most inviting smile. "I've never seen ticks out this early," she said encouragingly. "They usually lay low until later in the morning, when it's warmer."

"Last chance," Saxon warned with a laugh, turning Pink on his body and pulling her slippery wet ass into his groin. "If you don't come in, I'm going to fuck her without you."

The hard line of Danjer's mouth pulled down into a frown of disgust. "Go ahead without me. How can I hope to compete with *that* kind of sweet-talk?" He shook his head. "You sure know how to sweep a woman off her feet, Saxon."

Unabashed, Saxon laughed. "The girl doesn't seem to mind my sweet-talk."

"Maybe that's because she's still looking for protection," Danjer pointed out unkindly.

Almost before the words had left his mouth, Danjer wanted them back. Pink's lips turned downward as her smile faded. The knowledge that he'd made her unhappy made him feel incredibly uncomfortable. And he was feeling gloomy enough already — without feeling like an ass as well.

Fuck.

A golden bottomcrawler dragged itself out of the water, using its fins to pull its sleek, shimmering body up the sandy bank. He shifted his toe in its direction and it stopped, blinking at his boot and barking in a soft voice.

Saxon had caught Pink's expression, as well. "Fuck, Danjer. What did you say that for?"

But Pink lifted her chin with a proud smile returning to her small mouth. "No," she said swiftly, "Danjer's right. I *did* have an ulterior motive when I lured you into the water, Saxon."

"Lured *me*?"

She nodded. "I was hoping to get both of you naked so I could take advantage of two handsome gentlemen. But," she rested her gaze on Danjer, "since there's only one *gentleman* present, I guess it will just have to be you and me, Saxon."

Accent on gentlemen. Yeah. He got it. He picked up on that one right away.

Fuck.

"Did you hear that, Danjer?" Saxon prodded him with a smirk. "She called me a gentleman."

"Yeah?" he growled back. "Well, I guess you'd better take advantage of it, then. It's not likely to happen again anytime soon. We need to get back to Judipeao," he reminded his friend. "If you're going to fuck her, be quick about it."

Pulling his eyes away from the sight of their naked bodies fitted together, Danjer squinted into the sun. It wasn't just that he was being noble, although leaving the imp to his best friend did involve a certain amount of self-sacrifice. Okay — more than a certain amount. But while the noble side of him didn't want to interfere in Saxon's love life, the ignoble side of him really didn't want to share Pink.

Truth be said, Saxon's cavalier attitude toward the imp was irritating. Pink wasn't the sort of woman you *shared*. She wasn't the sort of woman you fucked with your friends. If he'd thought she meant no more than that to Saxon, he'd have kept her for himself. Scowling meanly, he wondered if it was too late to change his mind.

"You're no fun," Saxon grumbled, pulling away from the imp and turning her around to face him. From the corner of his eye, Danjer could see that his friend was now fully aroused, his cock swinging at the end of his torso in a huge, heavy arc. Saxon frowned down at his hard-on with an expression that would normally have made Danjer smile. Instead, he found his fists bunching into iron knots and his jaw clamped together so tightly he thought his molars would crack.

Fuck.

Trying not to watch, he turned his head, but that didn't stop him from seeing a lot more than he wanted to. He saw Saxon wrap both of Pink's hands around his massive erection. His friend's mouth was open and his hard jaw working as Saxon watched the dark head of his cock topping out above the pale wrap of Pink's fingers. Flexing the long muscles of his thighs, the sides of Saxon's ass dimpled as he thrust his hips to feed his cock into the wet tunnel of her hands.

Tiny pearls of water sparkled on the pale orbs of the imp's perfect breasts and Danjer swallowed hard. But it was the look on her face that really hurt. Her expression was a mixture of wonder and tenderness aimed at the man who shoved his cock through the clamp of her dainty fingers.

She looked both proud and pleased. She was *enjoying* Saxon's basely primal display of need. She was aroused by the fact that he was using her body to slake his carnal appetite. She wasn't doing this for Saxon because she felt sorry for him. And she wasn't doing this to get even with Danjer. If anything, she was doing this for herself.

"Oh, sweetheart," Saxon groaned as he pumped his hips at her and erupted onto her hands, coating her fingers with his shining semen as it shot from the slit in his flushed cock head. As he continued to feed his dick through her hands with the uneven jerk of his hips, his cum surged and spattered down between their bodies in thick drops.

As Danjer tightened his fists, Pink lifted a finger to her mouth. Her tongue darted out to curl over her fingertip, lapping at Saxon's cum as she graced the tall blond with an impish smile.

With a vicious snort Danjer ground his teeth.

In the next instant, Saxon lifted the imp by the waist and fell backward in the water, surfacing with a laugh and an arm sliding down her back. His hand cupped her cheeky bottom as he pulled her to her feet and guided her toward the bank.

Finding his feet, Danjer picked some lichen from the rock and threw it at the bottomcrawler, watching as the creature scuttled across the wet sand and gulped down the rumpled tatter of yellow vegetation. Turning, he straightened the aching flesh at his crotch and stooped to retrieve their pots and bowls from the water's edge. Flattening the metal ware against his leg, Danjer made his way up the path without waiting for Saxon and Pink. Seconds later, the laughing, dripping lovers raced past him toward the camp, their clothing bunched up in Saxon's huge fist. They were toweling themselves off by the time he joined them. Pink's short hair was almost dry, haloing her head in a glowing ruff.

With his face averted but his traitorous eyes sneaking over in Pink's direction, Danjer was more than a little surprised to find her forgiving smile directed at him. He had expected her to be annoyed with him. He tried hard to return her smile, knowing that it had to look more like a grimace than anything else.

"I don't want to impose on your kindness," she said, "nor burden you with my presence, but—"

"*Impose?*" Saxon blurted in protest, his voice muffled as he dragged the towel down his face. "*Burden?*" Silently, Saxon cut an accusing glance in his direction.

"When you were in the tavern, you said you fought for the Iron Duke," Pink continued tentatively as she pulled her tiny cotton shirt over her head. "Do you think you could get me in to see him? I thought I might take refuge at the Iron Palace."

Danjer frowned at this question, his eyes surfing the long line of her stomach — starting at the bottom edge of her shirt and sweeping down to the jewel that winked in the cup of her bellybutton. "We can get you in to see him," he grunted, trying to extract his eyes from the tangle of pale curls at the top of her legs. "I'm sure he'll be interested in your story."

She went on immediately, bending as she held her leggings and fed her feet into the top of her beige shorts. Danjer held his breath as he watched the lovely curve of her bottom sweep through her shapely thigh all the way to her bending knee. "When you attacked the Silver Duke, I saw an electrical discharge travel between your bikes."

Danjer nodded. "That's right."

"You killed those men."

"Yeah. Five hundred volts will do that to a guy," he said, swallowing hard as she pulled her pants up her legs and buttoned them closed.

"I've never seen a weapon like that before."

"Danjer built it," Saxon volunteered as he threw his towel at his bike and pulled on his jockstrap, arranging his sex inside the large pouch. "Did you notice the metal whips on our bikes?"

Slipping into her boots, Pink turned her head to gaze at their vehicles.

"Static collectors," he said, pulling on his leathers. "Danjer's trails on the ground and bleeds off electrons, giving his bike a net positive charge. At the same time, mine whips through the air and collects electrons, producing a negative charge. The bike stores the energy in an isolated insulator wafer. When we want to exchange a burst, we have only to get within twenty feet of each other. This slide," he said, approaching his bike and rapping a lever with his fist, "extends an antenna and directs the charge."

"In a pinch," Danjer added, "the collectors can also be used as a temporary energy source, to power our bikes."

Pink gazed at Danjer. "I'd heard Farthers were geniuses," she said.

Shifting his shoulders, Danjer made a face and shook his head. "Not geniuses," he corrected her, "just…inventive."

"In addition," Saxon went on, "he's built in a storm navigation system that senses electron concentration and guides the bikes around lightning strikes just before they happen. So we can ride safely through electrical storms."

At this, Pink's jaw dropped. "You can ride through storms?"

Saxon nodded. "And he installed a tracking feature on my console that lets me locate his bike—in case we ever get separated. Check it out," he invited her and she stepped closer to inspect the small square screen set into his bike's console.

"That's…pretty inventive," Pink stated, a look of awe falling across her face.

"Yeah, it is," Saxon agreed proudly. "Right now, he's working on a sort of a voice recognition system that will start up his bike."

"Voice recognition?"

"Well. Sort of."

"It's more of a tone recognition system," Danjer corrected his friend. "The bike will lift off and come to me if it hears certain notes propagated in the correct sequence. Let me show you," he said, walking away from his bike, which was settled on the ground. Pulling in his bottom lip, he set his tongue against his top teeth and blew out a sequence of five discordant notes, after which the bike rose from the ground and sped toward him. For a few seconds Danjer stared down at his bike. "There have been times," he admitted wryly, "when I would have traded all of my ideas for a simple blastuka."

"Blastuka?"

"Guns," Danjer volunteered. "Most of the weapons on Earth are projectile weapons. A small explosive charge is set behind a piece of pointed metal. When the charge explodes, the projectile travels a great distance very quickly, destroying everything in its path."

"Explodes...like a balloon full of air?"

"Kind of," Danjer told her. "But more powerful. This planet doesn't have the necessary compounds to produce explosive materials. Neither does it have fossil fuels," he continued. "Not that you need them here on eYona. The planet has a natural abundance of electrical activity which your ancestors learned to harness, store and utilize efficiently. And an electromagnetic drive is a better, cleaner way to travel than the fuel-driven vehicles on my planet. In addition, the magnetite in the planet's crust creates the perfect circumstances for magnetic field repulsion, allowing vehicles to hover, avoiding huge losses to friction.

"But," he went on to say, "if we had a few blastukas to replace our swords, we could end the war today. Of course, weapons trade between galaxies is strictly forbidden and the Inter-Gal penalties against smuggling are pretty severe."

Saxon snorted. "If you consider *internal parasitic torture* severe."

Straddling the bike, Danjer cupped his sex with his fingers, trying to make himself comfortable as he rearranged the heavy mass between his legs.

Pink licked her lips, and he didn't miss her guilty glance that slid to his crotch. His eyes caught on the tip of her tongue skimming over the shining blush of her mouth as she eyed his fingers tucked between his leathers and the bike's saddle.

With apparent effort, she dragged her eyes to his face. "Shall I ride with Saxon?" she asked him.

Grimly, he nodded back. "That would be a good idea," he told her soberly.

Chapter Seven

അ

Retracing their route northward, they made the Iron Duke's palace at mid-afternoon later that day. The gates swung open as they approached the walls and they sped through without halting, pulling up their bikes and leaving them in two of the yard's recharge slots as they climbed the palace stairs. Danjer nodded at the two men who flanked the palace's huge copper-banded doors and the guards hurried to pull them open for the small party. Turning left inside the palace doors, Danjer led the way through the entry to a large archway that opened into the great hall.

There was a scuff of boots on the stone stairs behind them. A glimpse of glinting auburn brushed with silver identified the Iron Duke in no uncertain terms.

"Didn't you guys get my message?" The duke grinned as he hurried down the long, winding staircase that dominated the entry.

"Sorry," Danjer threw over his shoulder as he continued into the hall and headed for a carved stone credenza topped with an impressive display of cut glass and sparkling crystal. There, he sorted through the Duke's many fine bottles. Frowning at a label, he removed the stopper from one and pulled four glasses forward to splash a measure of liquor into each squat tumbler. "We got sidetracked."

As Danjer poured out the golden liquor, sunlight beamed into the long room through small gothic windows set high on the gray stone walls. The long stretches of somber blocks were brightened here and there with colorful hangings and vertical strips of white neon lighting.

Like the queen's palace at Iverannon, the Iron Palace was an ancient structure constructed from massive blocks of solid stone. Unlike the newer palaces built in the last century, *this* palace was built for defense rather than beauty. Perhaps the only change the elegant old building had ever undergone was the replacement of its cold stone floors with a pour of golden styrowood.

Danjer liked it. He felt at home here, entrenched inside the thick stone walls.

Saxon helped himself to two of the glasses, turning to put one in Pink's hand.

"Did we miss much?" Danjer asked as he put a glass in the duke's hand.

"Yeah, you did! The Lady got drunk and was dancing on the table. When she started into the dance of the seven veils, I had to send her upstairs."

Lifting one dark eyebrow, Danjer's mouth twitched with a grin. "Did you go upstairs with her?"

"What do you think?" the older man responded with a laugh. "You should have been here. She made that Earth dish for dinner, Danjer. Spattaghi?"

"Spaghetti," Danjer corrected him with a warm smile.

"I think she was a little put out that you weren't here. I hope you're prepared to make it up to her."

Danjer pulled back his shoulders. "I'll do my best," he sighed while sporting a sly grin. His eyes snagged on Pink's apprehensive expression. "The Lady is the duke's wife," he explained, lowering his head to hers in a private aside.

Now she looked confused as well as apprehensive. Her gaze shuttered between the duke and Saxon and himself.

"He wouldn't let either of us *touch* her," Danjer added in a reassuring whisper.

The duke was smiling at Pink as he ran a hand through the silver hair at his temple. "I can see how you might have gotten sidetracked," he told the men while gazing at her approvingly. "I'm Au'Banner, by the way."

"The Iron Duke," she stammered, extending her hand.

He took her hand and placed it over his heart.

"Don't let The Lady catch you doing that," Saxon advised. "Oops," he muttered, "too late." Depositing his glass on the credenza, he moved to greet the woman entering the hall. With an arm hooked around her waist, Saxon dragged her into a hearty embrace punctuated with a resounding kiss. Her black, waving hair hung over his arm as her body curved against his.

"Is it just me, Saxon," she complained when he let her up for air, "or are you always hard?"

"It's just you," he asserted as he released her with a grin. "I don't know why you waste your time with Au'Banner when you could have…"

"Someone like Danjer?" she finished for him. "I don't know why I bother with the fickle bastard either. After all these years, you'd think he'd know better than to chat up the competition so long as there's a chance I might catch him at it. So long as he knows he could lose his hand…*or* his heart."

Although the woman was garbed in a long flowing gown that swished quietly against the styrowood floor, she carried herself with a lithe grace. And Danjer knew that she was more than able to carry out this threat against her husband. Not that she would. The Lady was in love with the duke.

Moving across the room with Saxon, The Lady smiled at Pink. "I'm Chloe," she introduced herself. "Au'Banner's wife."

The duke let Pink's hand fall. "I lost my heart six years ago," he reminded his wife, while arching his eyebrow for emphasis, "when I met *you*."

"Keep talking like that," she told him as she poured herself a drink, "and I might let you keep that hand."

"Good idea," he countered immediately. "It *might* come in handy later on."

"Oh," she answered breezily. "I'll make damn *sure* it does."

Pink laughed and Danjer found his gaze drawn to her mouth as all that wonderful sound spilled from her lips. "This is Pink," he said when he finally thought to introduce her. "She has a story that will interest both of you." He caught Pink's eye. "Perhaps she'll tell you about it at dinner, if she's not too tired."

Pink smiled at him and murmured, "Thank you."

"So you enjoyed your month's leave," the duke prodded Danjer with a smile and a glance at the imp.

"The men needed it," Danjer answered diffidently, ignoring his host's innuendo. "It's been a long time since we got a break. My cavalry should be drifting back in here over the next few days."

Danjer guided Pink across the room and deposited her on a long, low settee. "Any trouble while we were gone?" he asked, throwing himself into a wide, comfortable chair beside Pink.

The duke shook his head in answer. "I'll bring you up to date at dinner. You're staying the night, aren't you?"

"If you have room for us. I don't imagine Pink will want to spend the night in the men's barracks."

"Why would you assume that?" Pink cut in quickly with a small, daring smile.

In return, he gave her a dark smile of warning.

"Yeah, why would you think that?" Saxon taunted him from where he'd settled on the couch beside Pink. "It's not as though *you* haven't spent the night in the *women's* barracks."

"You ought to know," Danjer pointed out dryly, "being as you were with me at the time."

"I only came in looking for you," Saxon argued amiably.

"Yeah?" Danjer snorted. "Well it was amazing how long it took you to find me."

Saxon smiled. "Five hundred women can be a little distracting," he allowed.

Danjer made a point of ignoring him. "D'you have room for us?" he asked the duke.

Au'Banner grinned. "How much room do you need?" he queried, arching a suggestive eyebrow as his eyes traveled from Danjer to Saxon to the girl.

"Three rooms," Danjer answered while Saxon uttered "Two" in the same breath and Pink said "One" at the same time. Danjer smiled flatly. "Three rooms," he told the duke.

During dinner, the duke gave Saxon and Danjer a brief update on the war while the evening storms swept across the land and followed the sun into the west. The five of them were grouped around one corner of the dining hall's long banquet table—a huge slab of black marble flecked with stringers of white quartz. Thick wooden posts spaced at intervals along its incredible length supported the heavy slice of polished stone. The duke's kitchen staff had set several steaming dishes on the table before they'd disappeared, inconspicuously and discreetly. Only recently risen to power and unaccustomed to grandeur, the duke prized his privacy and maintained a remarkably small staff at the Iron Palace.

"So it's been quiet, then," Danjer summarized as Au'Banner finished his report.

Au'Banner nodded. "The queen is holding tight in Iverannon. We're the first line of defense. We're to fall back to the north if the baroness continues her invasion. Of course," he added, "I'd rather not do that."

Danjer grimaced as he settled his eyes on the contorted glass sculpture dominating the center of the polished tabletop. The product of a single lightning bolt and a great deal of black sand, the dark piece of natural art represented an unusually large and hot electrical discharge. Shaped roughly like an irregular star with blunted points, he smiled as he imagined

Pink clobbering the Silver Duke with a similar piece at the Copper Palace.

He interpreted Au'Banner's statement to mean that the stubborn Northman had no intention of retreating without a fight. But Iverannon was located on the edge of a steep bluff, the palace walls high and thick. If the baroness attacked, that was the ideal place to stage the Northern Alliance's final resistance. After two years of fighting, the North's remaining forces would have to unite and put forward a strong defense if they hoped to repel the baroness's army.

Retreat and regroup was their best option.

"She's up to something," The Lady stated. "The baroness. She's up to something."

Danjer's eyes swung to The Lady as he nodded his agreement. "Which brings us to Pink," he spoke up.

Encouraging Pink to relate her story to the duke and his wife, Danjer leaned back in his chair, quietly regarding the imp as she revealed the baroness's plot. He could have retold the story himself, but this ploy allowed him to watch her lovely, fey features as she talked. It gave him an excuse to settle his gaze on her face without looking like he was outright staring.

"You're lucky you ran into these two," The Lady told Pink as her tale drew to a close.

Pink nodded. "I was working my way north when we…became acquainted. I was trying to get here, to Judipeao."

Danjer dragged his eyes from Pink as he roused himself to speak. "So," Danjer leaned forward with his elbows on the table and his hands fisted into a loose knot. "It's important that we offer the girl protection," he stated.

"Agreed," the duke clipped out as he frowned at Pink. "We could send her to Iverannon with a message for the queen. Iverannon's lift station is still operational. They could flash Pink to the orbiting spaceport and put her on a ship off-planet."

"I don't think that will be necessary," Danjer countered without thinking. Then he had to stop and come up with a reasonable argument for *why* this might not be a good idea. "The baroness will be watching the spaceport," he offered lamely.

Help arrived unexpectedly from Saxon. "Personally, I have no intention of entrusting Pink's safety to anyone outside this room," he stated as he stretched in his chair.

Danjer nodded to himself. That pretty well summed up his own reaction to the idea. Saxon had articulated what Danjer couldn't bring himself to say.

"Right." Au'Banner inclined his chin. "I'll post extra guards on the walls as well as around the palace perimeter. We'll put Pink in that little room upstairs at the end of the corridor — the one with no windows or doors leading outside. You and Saxon can take your usual rooms. If anyone wants the imp, they'll have to come through all of us before they can get to her." Shoving his chair back, the duke got to his feet, yawning. "Your rooms are ready. Take yourselves off to bed whenever you like."

The Lady stood with her husband. "Please make yourself at home, Pink. If you need anything, Saxon and Danjer know their way around. They have full run of the palace."

"We do?" Saxon feigned surprise. "In that case, you won't mind if we get into your pants?"

Au'Banner growled as he put himself between Saxon and his wife.

"Because I'm guessing Pink will need some clothing," Saxon continued with an innocent smirk that fooled no one, "*if* you have anything you can spare, My Lady."

"I'll send some things to Pink's room," The Lady offered, rolling her eyes and shaking her head as she pulled her husband out of the room.

In the minutes that ticked by after the duke and his wife had gone up to bed, a still, expectant hush settled across the hall. The loud, oppressive cloak of silence was wrought with deep, sexual undertones. The night was late and there were bedrooms waiting for them on the upper floor. Bedrooms and beds—the natural setting for sex-ridden nights, rumpled sheets and tangled limbs. Straining bodies wrapped around each other, driving and pumping, lean naked groin pressed to soft, full pussy.

At that heavy instant in time, it felt as though the entire universe revolved around the need pulsing hot and urgent in Danjer's groin. Images and ideas intruded to possess his mind and overwhelm his every thought. A woman beneath him. Warm and pliant, damp and dusted with shimmering sweat, bending for him, shafted on his cock as he held her thrall to his needs, controlled in his uncompromising grasp. A woman gazing up at him from behind a pale curtain of yellow hair.

Jeezis Skies.

Sex and the imp. It was all he could think about.

When he finally took in a lungful of air, he realized he hadn't been breathing. Like an unstrung youth, he searched for a place to put his eyes, unwilling to let them wander too far toward the imp. Briefly, his gaze swept across Saxon's face, where he found his friend's expression just as dark and hungry as he knew his own must be—knew Saxon's blood was thundering through his veins in a pounding rush of desire and arousal, weighing heavy in his groin and pumping into his dick with every aching breath he drew. He knew Saxon was suffering as badly as he was, ridden with an edgy male need and consumed by one overwhelming purpose—to get between a woman's legs and pull them wide, get his cock deep inside her, fill her with dick and loose his cum inside the steamy hot clench of her cunt.

All he could think about was fucking her.

Fucking Pink.

Saxon moved first, pulling Pink up beside him as he stood. "I'm for bed," he announced in a tight, strained rumble.

As though in pain, he rubbed the heel of his palm down the front of his leather pants. Eyes narrowed, Danjer focused on his friend's thick fingers as Saxon plucked at the square diamond set at the base of his fly.

In a dark haze of sexual need, Danjer pushed himself to his feet. When Saxon moved Pink across the room, Danjer followed them up the long, winding staircase and along the carpeted corridor to the small interior bedroom the Duke had suggested for Pink.

Disengaging herself from Saxon, Pink lingered in the corridor while Saxon sauntered into the room which was to be hers. From his place in the middle of the hallway, Danjer could see the big blond inside *her* room, loosening his sword belt. Saxon's tall body was framed in the rectangular doorway and Danjer didn't like the picture one bit. Something deep inside him rebelled at the image, tightening his gut and tensing his jaw.

"Danjer," Pink said softly.

Her words startled him as she reached out to put her fingers on his forearm. But he pulled away before she could touch him. He shook his head grimly. "You made your choice," he told her. "At the river today." He took a steadying breath. "And it was the right one."

She shook her head. "I made my *choices*," she corrected him quietly. "You told me how you feel about Saxon and I understand. He's your best friend. But...I was hoping you'd join us in the river."

Her words sucked at his soul and licked up the long length of his raging hard-on, as though her hot mouth were wrapped around his cock and pulling heartlessly at his flesh. Briefly, his eyes closed as he felt himself go thermo-nova—wanting her but not wanting her like that. "I'm not like that," he told her warningly, pulling away and turning.

"I am," she insisted bravely. "No, stop, Danjer. Let me explain. Imps are…made for two men. Try to understand. It's not only emotional. It's physical."

He felt her fingers brush his forearm again and the next thing he knew, she was against the wall, beneath him. "*Don't* touch me," he rasped, forcing the words through his clenched teeth. "Or you'll soon learn more about Earthers than you'd ever wish to know. None of which you'd enjoy. Do you understand me, girl? I don't know what you're used to but I doubt it includes getting reamed by uncivilized barbarians from backworld planets."

He felt her go stiff as he glared down at her. Her eyes burned up at him as her small palms pushed against his chest. "How bad could it be?" she shot back. "I don't see how it could be any worse than what happened to me at the Copper Palace. Exactly how pleasant do you think that was, Danjer?"

Now it was his turn to still. Ah, fuck. Apology coming up right here.

"Fuck," he said. "I'm sorry, Pink."

But he didn't move. He didn't think he *could* move. It felt too damn good, pressed up against her. He had her crammed up against the wall, her slender body pinned beneath his, her lovely plump breasts crushed beneath his chest, her firm belly cradling the taut length of his cock. He ached to take her. Ached with a gut-grinding need that had him in knots.

The sensation of her firm flesh pressed tight against his own, so close, separated only by their layered clothing, was enough to make him spill right then and there, inside his leathers. He wanted to rock into her, drive against her, somehow leave his mark on her. Pulling in a raw gasp, he gripped her hips and flexed his knees to drag his cock over her belly one time. Together, they moaned, their voices tangling together, low and throaty, deep and throttled, tortured with an overpowering need that couldn't be slaked standing fully clothed against a wall.

Slowly, he dragged his cock against her belly again, thrusting his hips to burrow his cock head deep in her flesh.

"Other than that," she said beneath a low moan, "I haven't had a whole lot of experience. A few kisses. A little petting. One man who couldn't satisfy me."

Lost in the male urge to pump and penetrate, Danjer's first impulse was to ignore this comment. Conversation had never *in his lifetime* seemed so difficult. He used his tongue to track the delicate shell of her ear before sucking her earlobe between the nipping clamp of his teeth. Eventually, her words battled their way through the thick fog of lust that wrapped his brain. With an extraordinary amount of difficulty, he pushed away from her enough to look down on her face.

"Only one man? And The Silver Duke? Only that...*beast* with his glass and rubber?"

As if to shield herself from the memory of the Silver Duke, her eyelids covered her green gaze for an instant. When she opened her eyes, her gaze lifted to burn up at him proudly. "And Saxon," she told him almost defiantly. "In the river."

Ah yes, Saxon. She wouldn't let him forget Saxon—no matter how much he wanted to at this precise moment in time. His muscles tightened before his shoulders slumped at his own meanness. Poor kid. Giving Saxon a hand job this morning was her best sexual experience to date. And she hadn't even gotten off.

The green glow of her gaze continued to burn up at him.

Damage control.

"How is that possible?" he demanded. "You're so...lovely."

Her head tipped down. He felt her smile curling against the deep bole at the base of his neck, and he knew he'd scored with the flattery defense.

"I've had my chances," she admitted, "but...would you have casual sex, if you were me? Think about it. I'm like a walking lethal weapon. I threaten every man who lies with me.

"And what about me?" she murmured. "If a man were to kiss me, accidentally or otherwise, I'd be stuck with him, trailing me around helplessly for the rest of my life. I wouldn't take a man—or men—unless I was certain I could live with them forever...if I had to."

In the unfilled silence that followed, he felt her lips brush up his neck and nudge against his jaw. His reaction to this impetus was pure male instinct. He reached for her without thinking, covering her lips with his, driving his tongue into the damp heat of her mouth as his hands moved to her face and he held her head, mining her mouth for every erotic sensation he could find there, forcing his tongue to the back of her throat as she fought back with the stroke and give of her own serpentine caresses.

Fuck, he wanted her. He began to grind his hips against her in an instinctive male urge for satisfaction. A few more scraping thrusts and he'd be there. "Pink," he groaned breathlessly into her mouth. "Oh Jeezis, Pink, I..."

"What are you two doing?"

Danjer froze, his eyes widening with sudden sanity as he heard Saxon's voice behind him. Pink gazed up at him, her eyes half closed, slumberous with arousal. Planting his hands against the wall, Danjer separated himself from the woman he was sealed against. Strangely, he felt like he was leaving a huge part of himself behind. The most important part. A part of himself he really couldn't do without.

Something dark and deep and emotionally dangerous welled up in its place.

"What are you two doing?" Saxon repeated as Danjer turned to face his friend, standing in the open doorway to Pink's room. "And why are you doing it without me?" Saxon shook his head at them as he smiled tentatively, his eyes shuttling uncertainly between the two of them.

Danjer felt Pink's hand wrap around his wrist. Tender warmth overtook her expression as she gazed at Saxon.

How could she do that? How could she look at Saxon that way after kissing him…the other way? Why did he feel so betrayed? It wasn't her fault. He'd just about pushed her into Saxon's arms. He had no right to be angry. If anything, it was he who was betraying Saxon.

Shaking free of Pink, he forced a smile onto his lips. "Just warming her up for you," he told Saxon stiffly.

Saxon jerked his chin upward as though he understood. Reaching for the bottom edge of his wrap, he pulled it over his head then stretched his huge shoulders and flexed his bulging muscles like a great golden cat. The act, though carried out with a smile, looked like both a mating display as well as a challenge for possession of the slender female caught between the two men.

Okay, Saxon. Got it. He could take a hint. He wasn't stupid, just horny.

Taking the first difficult step away from Pink, Danjer made his feet carry him the several paces to his bedroom door. Resisting the urge to rip the door off its hinges, he yanked it open then gave it a vicious jab with his elbow as he entered the room. The door closed with a crashing slam.

Immediately, his cock was out and in his hand as he wrapped his long fingers around his shaft and stroked out its dark, ridged length. Striding for the slashroom, he pulled brutally on his dick, only just reaching the marble counter before he flashed and came, his semen splashing onto the slightly curving countertop. Staring blankly at his cum as it surged onto the counter, he muffled a groan that hurt too much to voice. His chin dropped and his shoulders sagged. Leaning one hand against the wall, he palmed a flat button and watched the curtain of shimmering cleansers slash through the air along the length of the counter. For several seconds, he stared at his unhappy reflection in the mirror. His gaze blazed a bright defiant blue before he closed his eyes and hung his head in defeat.

This wasn't working. He needed to get away—from Saxon and Pink—before his need to possess the imp destroyed his relationship with the greatest friend he'd ever known.

Chapter Eight

ଈ୬

The thought of Saxon on top of Pink kept Danjer tossing all night. The thought of Pink with her eyes half-closed, her lips curled into a wanton smile and those long shapely legs wrapped around Saxon's hips as he rode into her...

Jeezis Skies. Pushing himself out of bed in the gray dawn, Danjer padded across the bedroom on his way to the slashroom. Stepping into the slashstall, he stretched his arms and locked his fingers behind his neck. His weight on the floor of the stall activated the cool slash of cleansers. Closing his eyes, Danjer let the liquid curtain slash across him several times more than necessary before he stepped out of the stall. After toweling himself off, he dressed in a white wrap and black leathers before he headed down the stairs.

His long stride faltered as he entered the dining hall and realized Saxon was seated at the marble table that dominated the room. Despite the fact that he was a huge man, Saxon looked diminished, somehow — strangely forlorn and alone as he sat, taking up only a tiny portion of the enormous banquet table. Saxon shifted in his seat and his reflection stirred on the still, black surface of the polished tabletop.

Glancing at his friend, Danjer poured himself a cup of char and lifted it to his lips as he turned back to face Saxon. The two men regarded each other across an incredible length of silence.

Finally Saxon smiled wanly. "What's wrong?" he queried.

"Nothing," Danjer bit off in a quiet word, taking another long sip of the scalding brew, welcoming the burn as it traveled his tight throat.

"You look about as happy as I feel."

Holding his breath, Danjer tilted his head and gave Saxon a questioning look.

"She wouldn't have me...last night."

Expelling the breath lodged in his lungs, Danjer grabbed at the counter behind him, steadying himself with one hand before taking another sip of char. "I thought you spent the night with her."

Saxon shook his head. "I spent the night in the room across the hall from yours." The blond's expression was a bit hopeless as he shook his head. "I don't know what went wrong. After what happened at the river yesterday, I thought I was in!"

Running both hands through the tangled silk of his hair, Saxon grimaced and said in a hard rush, "I'm crazy about her. I...I wish I could tell her. But—" He broke off, swallowing as his hands fisted on the dark surface of the table, "You know how I am with words...ever since D'Almiers."

Danjer looked at the ground, nodding his head as he was swamped to his knees in soul-strafing, crushing, debilitating remorse.

When he blinked at the lines on the styrowood floor, he could see Saxon. *Saxon lying white and unconscious on the sandy ground, his blood terrifyingly dark, welling up through the ragged split in his helm.*

Saxon had saved his life when he'd taken that blow for Danjer. His friend had lived but had been somewhat disoriented ever since. Previously sharp and self-assured, the easygoing warrior now got turned around easily. And in a world with few roads to point the way, a sense of direction was almost a necessity. In addition to the disorientation Saxon suffered, he also had trouble expressing himself.

Saxon had sacrificed all this for him.

For a long time, Danjer stared at the floor, unwilling to meet Saxon's eyes.

There was a patter of light feet on the stairs and both men lifted their heads. Danjer watched his friend's gaze fix on the stairs beyond the wide double entry of the dining hall.

"Here she comes," Saxon muttered. His eyes swung back to Danjer's. "I need to tell her," he blurted suddenly. "Will you help me?"

With a grimace of reluctance, Danjer turned his face. "I'll do my best," he told Saxon with grating determination. This wasn't going to be easy. Reaching for a cup and filling it with the steaming brew, he forced a smile onto his face. "Don't get mad at me if she takes it the wrong way," he grumbled with a taunting growl. Crossing the room to the table, he pulled out a chair for Pink as she entered, placing the char before her as she sat.

She looked both fresh and winsomely wild, dressed in a short off-white stretchy top that hugged her breasts and left her midriff bare. On her hips hung a pair of The Lady's soft suede leggings. As Pink was slimmer than Chloe, the pants slouched low on her hips, displaying the jewel which twinkled in her bellybutton.

"Pink," Saxon started immediately, "I need to tell you something. It's…important."

Her eyes traveled cautiously between the two men as she pulled her chair underneath her and Danjer returned to his post by the char generator.

"It's about you and me, and how I feel about you. I want to…" helplessly, he looked to his friend leaning against the counter.

"Fuck you," Danjer supplied.

"No!"

"Lay you?" was his next suggestion.

"*No!*" Saxon glared at his friend, and Danjer relented with a wry smile.

"Make love to you."

"Yes!" Saxon almost shouted. "I want to make love to you, Pink. Ever since I met you, I've wanted you. You're all I can think of. I've never been so...attracted to a woman. You're so..."

"Beautiful," Danjer said quietly.

"Yes," Saxon agreed. "And more than that, you're..."

"The loveliest creature I've ever set eyes on."

Saxon nodded as he stared at the imp imploringly.

"You're warm and considerate and kind and brave. When you're near," Danjer continued, "it's all I can do to keep my hands off you. It's all I can do to *breathe*," he whispered. "When you laugh, I want it to last forever."

Saxon frowned as his gaze swung up to his friend's face.

"I want to be the man who makes you laugh, who touches you and makes love to you. I want to be the man who wakes up next to you, every day for the rest of my life. I want you in my bed. In my home. In my world. I want you in my life. For as long as I live."

"Damn," Saxon whispered. There was an awkward silence as Saxon stared at Danjer while Danjer gazed across the room at Pink. Pink's eyes remained downcast, fixed on her steaming cup, her lips caught between her teeth.

Abruptly, Danjer shook himself. "Is that what you meant to say?" he asked Saxon without looking at him.

"Yeah," Saxon returned quietly. "Yeah...that pretty much covers it."

"I'll leave you two alone," Danjer said quickly, turning to stride stiffly through the door. The hard sound of his cleats grew distant as he paced down the corridor.

Saxon watched the empty doorway for several moments. "Fuck me for an idiot," he said raggedly, staring at the opening. He glanced toward the girl across the corner of the table. "Do you feel the same way about him?"

With her teeth still buried in her bottom lip, Pink raised her haunted gaze to his.

He stood suddenly. "Damn," he said, "*I'm* the one who should be leaving."

"No," she said quickly. "Danjer wouldn't want that, Saxon. I wouldn't want that. I *won't* come between you and your best friend. Besides," she said, shaking her head as she gazed into her lap. "I love *you*, too."

Frowning at her, Saxon shook his head.

"I do," she said in a low voice. "Danjer doesn't understand how that could be true." She raised her eyes to Saxon's. "Imps are made for two lovers. I think I could make him understand if I could just get him into bed. But he won't. He won't betray your friendship." Her white teeth sank into her lower lip, and the look in that shadowed gaze revealed her frustration and misery.

"I was hoping he'd join us in the river. If he had, I might have had a chance to show him—to show you both—how I feel about you. How I need both of you."

Saxon stared at her finger, dragging at a bead of water and tracing a long, narrow figure eight on the table's polished black surface. "Imps are made for two lovers," she told him helplessly, shaking her head again. "I don't know how else to explain it."

Pushing his chair back with a hurried scrape, Saxon clamped a huge fist around Pink's wrist and strode from the room, towing the girl behind him.

Danjer's bike was gone when they reached the yard. Saxon lifted Pink onto his bike as it rose into the air. Straddling the bike, he flipped on his tracking device and set the console to follow. Saluting the guards across the yard, they glided through the huge gates as they opened.

Even pushing the bike to maximum speed, it took over an hour to catch up to Danjer, who finally stopped when he realized they were behind him. As his bike dropped to the ground, the dark man stalked away into a sparsely populated grove of tall, gangly tallic trees. The trees were naked, devoid of branches, their bark incredibly smooth and gleaming with a polished surface. Struck often by lightning, the trees survived by imbuing metal into their bark so that the electricity coursed down the outside of the tree without harming the living center. A thick bundle of leaves grew from a mass of green shoots that bunched at the very crown of the tree as well as in a thick cluster around the base.

"Stay here," Saxon told Pink, leaving her beside the bikes and heading off through the widely spaced trees to intercept his friend.

"Danjer," he called, and his friend spun around to face him. Danjer's expression was harried and frustrated as he glared at Saxon. "I know what you're doing," Saxon told him. "You're a good friend, Danjer," he said quietly.

Danjer turned away from him, ripping his hands through the rumpled silk of his shining black hair.

"Danjer," Saxon grated, fumbling for the next words. "You can't just...leave me. Leave us. My...sense of direction is a bit off. It has been ever since—"

"Don't make me feel guilty, Saxon," Danjer cut in, turning again to face him. "You'll be all right without me. You'll have Pink to keep track for you."

Saxon nodded as he stared at the ground searchingly. "So you love me enough to give her up—for my sake." Again he nodded before he lifted his gaze to connect with Danjer's. "But do you love me enough to share her with me?"

Danjer froze. "*Don't* make me feel guilty, Saxon."

"Fuck, Danjer. She doesn't love me. Not really. Not like she does you! Do you love me enough to share her with me, Danjer?" he continued rapidly, his words tumbling over themselves. "It's not like it doesn't happen. It's not as though it's unheard of. There are plenty of...of multi-relationships.

Some of them even work," he argued. "I've an uncle who has two wives. They're happy!"

"Yeah, well it wouldn't work for me."

"Why not?"

"Because I don't feel that way about her!" Danjer exploded. His brilliant eyes were wild, his breathing uneven as he stared at Saxon. "Because I'm an Earther!" he shouted, jabbing his thumb into his chest. "Earthers don't share their women."

"Never?"

"Not if they...care about them," Danjer ground out through clenched teeth.

"Not if they love them?" Saxon asked quietly but Danjer didn't answer. "What happens when two friends love the same woman?"

"Then," Danjer grunted, averting his gaze, "they're not friends anymore."

"*What?*" Saxon asked with quiet panic. "*What?*"

"You heard me."

"Yeah, I heard you. I just don't believe you. Are Earthers really that fucked up?"

A high-pitched scream cut their argument short.

As one, both men stiffened, their eyes locked on each other. Then, turning, they sprinted toward the place where they'd left their bikes. What they found beyond the tallicwood grove was enough to give a brave man pause—but neither of them hesitated for an instant—instead, their cleats dug into the sandy soil as they threw themselves across the open ground to get to the imp.

A giant tick had the girl in its fore pincers as its stiff dark wings rustled open for flight. Nearby, a wide depression in the sandy ground marked the creature's recent bed where it had lain, concealed beneath a blanket of warm black sand.

Pink trailed her feet on the ground, digging in her booted heels, struggling within the bloodsucker's grasp. As the men charged after her, the bottom cuff of her loose leggings snagged on a groundwood twig and for a moment the tick stalled, anchored in mid-air, as it dipped toward the ground. The next moment, Pink's feet swung into the air and the ugly behemoth was airborne—though only by a few inches. Danjer hurtled onward, racing to catch the tick, while Saxon veered off toward his bike.

Leaping into the air, Danjer caught at the trailing end of a spindly rear leg and the tick hit the ground once then bounced back into the air. Danjer cursed as he stared for one instant at the broken limb still jerking in his fist, then he flung it aside as he again launched himself at the flying arachnid.

Twenty feet away, Saxon punched his bike to life as his friend scrambled to get a grip on the slick, rounded surface of the tick's hard, polished wing. Fighting, grappling and dragging his feet all at the same time, Danjer slowed the tick's rate of departure as it headed out into the empty sand wastes.

Screaming after his companions, Saxon hunched over his console as he raced to catch them. Coming alongside the evil monstrosity, he locked his left foot in the stirrup as he stood with his other boot on the saddle. With his sword drawn, he sped across the sand, hacking at the tick where the base of its thick fore pincer met its ugly maw, trying to free the girl from its grip. At the same time, Danjer plunged his sword between the monster's spread wings and buried it to the hilt as he ripped downward. Thick, sticky blood welled out of the wound and, like a listing ship, the flying tick veered toward the ground while the two men continued to hack and slash.

"She's off!" Saxon shouted as a final driving cut severed the wide pincer that held the girl, and Pink dropped to the dark sand. Upon hearing this, Danjer gave up his grasp on the tick's thick, hard wing and slipped from the animal's back.

Dropping into his saddle and wheeling the bike around, Saxon guided his magnabike to Danjer's side. Together they watched the creature wobble through the air then plow into the ground in a huge, surfing spray of sand. The wrecked monster rolled onto its side and its legs jerked feebly in the air a few times before Danjer threw himself on the bike behind Saxon. Together, they accelerated toward the girl now sitting in the sand a hundred feet behind them.

The bike was shushing to a halt as the men jumped to the ground and ran the few remaining steps toward her. Danjer reached her first, tearing the jointed claw from her waist and yanking her into his arms. For several heartbeats, he clutched her tightly before he pulled her face out of his chest. With her pale cheeks trapped in the cradle of his tremoring hands, he kissed her—hard, hungrily and passionately. And only let up when he realized Saxon stood just beyond Pink, his fists clenching as his hands hovered at his sides.

With sudden comprehension, Danjer took her by the shoulders and pushed her away a separating inch. His eyes burned down on her face, then at Saxon's as he tried to remove his clutching grip from her shoulders—tried to give her up to his best friend. But Saxon stepped forward and locked his own hands over Danjer's. "We'll not argue again," Saxon told him.

Darkly, with a growl building inside his chest, Danjer watched Saxon's lips descend to nip a line down the girl's neck before he finally returned his own lips to the clinging, moist heat of her mouth.

"I'll take the first watch," Saxon murmured and Danjer interrupted his kiss long enough to glower at his best friend as the man fell to one knee and worked Pink's pants down her legs. "Are you protected, Pink?" Saxon asked as he pulled her little boots from her feet.

When alarm filled her wide-eyed gaze, Danjer winced for her sake as well as his own. Protected or unprotected, at this point, there wasn't anything in this world that was going to stop him from fucking her.

"No. Don't worry, sweetheart. I have something." Backing away, Saxon turned and headed for his saddlecases. "What flavor do you want?" he asked Danjer as he strode back toward them, clutching a handful of paper-wrapped sticks in his fist.

"I don't care," Danjer breathed, his eyes clinging to the girl he held before him.

"What?"

"I don't care," he voiced more loudly, ripping his stained wrap over his head and using it to wipe the tick's yellow blood from his black leathers. "Anything. Natural," he answered on a moan. "I won't be tasting her," he complained as his shirt fell from his fingers and his mouth dipped to track a line along Pink's collarbone. When she gasped, his hands tightened around her waist, pulling her into his body and forcing her back to arch. Her nipples were tight little knots, stabbing at the soft fabric that wrapped her sweet round tits. All he could feel was her warm smooth flesh beneath his hands, her full breasts crushed beneath his chest, the tiny scratch of her belly ring on his leathers. All he could hear was her high, torrid pants overlain by the harsh rush of his own lust-roughened gasps. All he could think about was getting her on his cock.

"Easy," he heard Saxon say. Then, "Turn her."

"Saxon," Danjer urged breathlessly, turning her to face the other man. The blond's hand was under her thigh, sliding up along its smooth length as he lifted her knee. Apparently anxious to help, Pink stretched her leg out straight and rested her foot on Saxon's shoulder.

"I've got it," Saxon rasped, knotting both his hands in the front of her silky shorts and wrenching them apart. Then he stopped, an unwrapped desiccating stick in his hand as he stared into Pink's open pussy.

"Saxon," Danjer pleaded with a groan.

"Uh," Saxon hesitated, "where do you want it?"

A low snarl escaped his throat. "What do you mean, where do I want it?"

"I mean you have more than the usual number of choices," Saxon said quietly. "Look at this."

Taking Pink's foot from his shoulder, Saxon folded her leg at the knee and eased it to the ground. Then he scooped her into his arms and carried her to his bike. Lowering Pink to sit sideways on the smooth saddle, Saxon knelt before her. When Danjer followed, he pulled the Earther down to his knees beside him.

"Spread your legs, Pink," Saxon murmured huskily. "Spread your legs and show Danjer your pussy."

With her teeth in her bottom lip, she moved her legs apart and, with a hand on the inside of either thigh, Saxon helped her to get them wider. Then he eased his fingers either side of her seam and pulled her labia open.

Danjer grunted with surprise.

"This is what she's been trying to tell us. Isn't it, Pink?"

Shyly, she nodded as the two men stared into the parted lips of her sex...at the slender, hourglass shaped opening of her vagina. Pulling down on the base of her vulva, Saxon slipped the rounded head of a protective stick inside the lower half of the long figure eight, pushing the end gently until it disappeared. As the men gazed into her long, luscious opening, Saxon tore the wrapper off a second stick and eased it into her vagina above the first. Saxon tilted his head. "By the Princess, she smells delicious. Do you think...we could both get in there?"

"Not this time," Danjer growled, elbowing him aside with a feral glare.

Stumbling to his feet, Saxon looked on as Danjer quickly straddled the low bike, unclasped his weapons belt and threw it aside. Danjer opened his leggings, pulled out his cock and stroked his fist once down its long length. The dark, fat head was wet, shining as his pre-cum streamed from the neat slit at the top of his dick, coating his broad cock head with a glistening veil of slick moisture. Lifting Pink at the waist, Danjer turned her to face him as he lowered himself to sit on the bike's saddle. Holding her close, he tongued the fabric stretching over her nipples as he positioned her vagina over his cock.

Automatically, Saxon put his foot on the other side of the bike and supported her weight with his hands while he pulled her cheeks apart. "Give her a second for the protection to dissolve," he warned Danjer.

"You're on watch," Danjer reminded him with a growl, never removing his mouth from Pink's breasts.

Saxon nodded. "But I didn't say what I'd be watching." Saxon took a deep breath. "You're not doing this without me." Pulling his sword, he buried the tip into the sandy soil beside him, then he yanked at the clasp that closed his wide belt low on his hips. When his belt was undone, he eased it away from his body.

"What do you mean?" Danjer demanded, pulling his face out of Pink's chest and glaring over her shoulder at his friend.

"You're not fucking her without me," Saxon challenged quietly, opening his fly and guiding his dick out.

"No?" Danjer rasped. And with that word, he dropped Pink onto his cock.

Immediately, the imp went mad, screaming as she twisted wildly on his cock. Danjer's head tipped forward onto her bobbing breasts, his eyes blinking as he gulped several times under the racking pleasure the jumping imp effected on his sex. "Jeezis Skies," he groaned as he tried to hold her shimmying body on his dick. "What...what's wrong with you? Pink!"

"She's orgasming," Saxon told him bluntly.

Danjer gasped and gritted his teeth. "Already?" He stared at Pink's face. Her eyes had rolled back in her head and her expression was a wild mixture of anguish and pleasure. "This long? No woman orgasms for this long."

"She's not a woman. She's an imp."

Danjer grimaced. "At this rate, I'm not going to last two minutes. Jeezis," he cursed as he gulped in another breath.

Pink was making an abrupt series of short strangled noises that sounded a lot like sobs of distress. Blinking his eyes wide, Danjer pulled her off his cock. Immediately, she sagged against him, shuddering as her head fell forward to rest on the top of his. "Pink," he asked with careful awe, "are you all right?"

She groaned in answer, shaking her head against his hair. "Please. I need both of you." He felt a hot tear land on the tip of his cock, followed by the sliding press of her thumb as she smoothed the wet drop over his cock head. She sucked in several short breaths. "I don't know how to explain," she whispered. "When I'm on you...Danjer, it's like an electrical short circuit inside me, and I'm whipped around on the stark edge of pleasure, mad at the point of release but unable to close up and achieve satisfaction. I know it sounds ridiculous but I...I need two men to close the circuit and turn the light on."

Danjer blew out a surprised laugh while Saxon stood and rucked his leathers down his legs. Kicking off his pants and boots, Saxon skimmed his jockstrap over his thighs and let it drop to his feet.

When Pink tried to hide her face in Danjer's hair, he pulled her down onto the saddle, facing him.

"Does that make any sense at all?" she whimpered.

He lifted her chin with his fist. "That makes all the sense in the world...in this world, anyhow, where there's such an abundance of electrical energy," he told her. His gaze slid to Saxon, now standing naked behind her. The long masculine lines of Saxon's legs were neat and hard and burnished with fine golden hair. "Is…that why the Silver Duke couldn't make you come?

She gave him a tiny affirmative nod.

"Jeezis Skies," he said in sudden revelation. "The glass rods. The rubber…those are both nonconductive materials."

She tilted her head as she gazed into his eyes. Again she nodded.

"Conductors," he whispered with a gentle smile. "You need two conductors. Like penises or fingers or tongues. Water or maybe even metal. Something that has the ability to conduct."

Frowning thoughtfully, he looked back over the sand to the grove of trees where he'd left his bike. He blew out five shrill notes and watched his bike as it sped toward them. When the bikes were resting on the ground beside each other, separated by about three feet, he lifted Pink by the waist and held her between the two bikes. "Spread your legs, little imp," he told her, "and we'll close your circuit for you. That's it. Put your feet on the bikes' saddles."

As Saxon moved behind Pink and pulled her weight into his arms, Danjer took the time to draw the sword from his belt on the ground and plant its tip in the sand beside Saxon's. With both swords within arm's reach, Danjer dropped to his knees in front of Pink. "Saxon," he said. At this word, his friend moved her hips down his long body, guiding her to bend her knees and open her legs for Danjer. "Pull her cheeks open while I stroke her clit," Danjer told him.

Danjer took a breath and held it, watching the seam of her sex part as he pulled her labia open with his thumbs. Spreading her plump lips wide, he gazed up into the perfect pink of her pussy, her pretty ruffled folds damp around the dark center of her beckoning entrance. Swallowing hard, he repositioned his hand and brushed his thumb over her rumpled clitoris while his fingers kept her labia spread for his avid, violate gaze. Saxon tugged on the cheeks of her ass, stretching the rim of her vulva wide as a thin rivulet of moisture trickled from the base of her hourglass opening.

He longed to kiss her right there. Right where a woman was most captivating. Right where a woman ached for a man—and where a man ached to possess a woman. Jeezis Skies. The imp's liquid perfume, as it leaked from her cunt, was enough to drive a man to madness.

Pink's head fell back on Saxon's shoulder and Saxon mouthed the side of her neck hungrily as she closed her eyes and sighed with pleasure. As Danjer played with her pussy, spreading her lips and reveling in all her glistening pink secrets, Saxon's gaze burned down at him, his green eyes on fire as he followed his friend's every action.

Again and again, Danjer feathered the rough pad of his thumb over her clit, taking his time, relentlessly thorough, smiling ruthlessly when he heard Saxon swallow hard.

With his dick slotted up against the crease of her ass, Saxon moved his hips instinctively, dragging his cock up through the warm parting between her buttocks and Pink started to squirm, panting as she made small murmuring sounds of helpless pleasure.

Saxon was right. Pink's feminine whimpers filled Danjer with a nameless euphoria. There was nothing like a woman helpless in your hands, helpless on your dick. Only a woman could make you feel like this—like you could do anything. Anything in the world. Jeezis Skies. At that moment he felt like the most powerful bastard on the face of eYona.

"Danjer," Saxon finally groaned as he spread his legs and clamped the root of his cock. With his hand beneath his shaft, he fed his wide head between her legs, prodding eagerly at her opening.

Immediately Danjer stood to join his friend as he pushed his cock head through the front of her pussy, nudging through her sleek, satin folds, stopping when the tip of his cock settled against her soft warm notch. Saxon moved and the friction of

Saxon's silken cock head against his own sensitive flesh made him suck in a sudden gasp. Together they entered her, Saxon's hands covering Danjer's on Pink's waist as they forced her down onto their dicks.

She went wild on them, thrashing and calling and sobbing their names while they stared at each other, stunned with pleasure. Inside the imp's hot channel, their cocks were crowded together as her cunt sucked at their flesh in long, greedy, rippling swallows. "I can't believe we both fit," Saxon choked out. "By the Princess, I'm in her all the way to my balls."

"I know," Danjer gritted out. "They're crammed up against mine."

"I thought her openings were...separated," Saxon panted. "I didn't realize we'd be together in there." Saxon closed his eyes and then opened them again to stare over Pink's shoulder at Danjer. His gaze burned with a liquid green fire of pleasure. "Let's get fucked," he told Danjer and together they bent their knees and clamped her waist as they drove their hips upward into her climaxing cunt. Grunting and straining, they pulled their hips upward as they forced their cocks into her body and pulled her supple frame down to meet the brutal thrust of their hips.

Danjer's eyes were fixed on the base of his cock and Saxon's gaze was lowered to the place where he spread her cheeks, where the shining width of his thick root pistoned between her legs. With one leg inside his friend's and the other outside, the men flexed their knees together as they banged into her, arriving almost simultaneously as their balls tightened together like hard fruit. Their glans moved against one another, sliding and rubbing in an illicit male kiss at the same time Pink's vagina seized suddenly, clamping on their cocks with unbearable pressure and forcing their flesh together tightly as they emptied inside her.

"Fuck," Saxon breathed in whispered awe as the three of them stood strapped together, entwined like trees and vines. He gazed over Pink's shoulder at Danjer. "That was incredible.

"I have never come so hard before in my life. Pink's hot, tight cunt choking the life out of my dick. The smooth drag of your cock head riding my shaft, pounding against my..." he pushed out a hoarse groan. "Fuck," he said, shaking his head, apparently lost for more articulate words.

Danjer could only nod, his heart drumming in his chest, a lump of emotion filling his throat. Pink was still making small kitten-like noises. The purely female sounds of satisfaction made him smile. "I take it we got your light turned on," he whispered against her cheek.

"Mmm-hmm," she purred.

As Saxon nuzzled his face against Pink's temple and put a kiss on the side of her face, Danjer claimed her lips and drank in a deep kiss of completion. His fingers on Pink's waist were still caught beneath the hard snare of Saxon's thick digits and, despite the complete pleasure that still pounded through his veins, he resented the presence of Saxon's hands.

At the same time, he recognized that between him and Saxon, Saxon was the stronger man.

The stronger man by far.

Chapter Nine

ഔ

Feeling deliciously used and basking in a glow of stunned bliss, Pink slumped between the sex-damp bodies of her two warriors. She hadn't guessed sex could be like that. Her past experiences had done nothing to prepare her for this sort of consummate copulation. She'd never shared an orgasm with a man before. She hadn't known it would be so…intense. So satisfying. So fulfilling. Talk about closure! Her cunt closing on those two magnificent cocks was surely the high point of her life.

She could tell right now, she was going to need more high points.

Lots more high points, she thought, as a warm glow of satisfaction burned through her blood.

She was contemplating seducing a repeat performance out of the two men, when Saxon shifted behind her, his huge frame stiffening as he turned his head. "Danjer," he warned quietly.

Danjer lifted his lips from the corner of Pink's mouth as he turned to follow Saxon's gaze out across the sand. Disengaging himself from the sweaty tangle of limbs, Danjer rearranged his sex beneath his jockstrap and closed his leathers as he moved to stand between his friends and the silently approaching bikes. As he stood with legs spread, he dragged his sword out of the ground, sheathed it in one long thrust and belted it around his hips.

At the same time, Saxon dug Pink's leggings out of the sandy soil and shielded the imp as she pulled her pants up her legs. He was reaching for his own leathers as the dozen bikes swept down on them.

Apprehensively, Pink glanced at Saxon's face then relaxed when the curving line of his mouth widened into a grin.

Danjer sauntered toward the bikers while Saxon tightened his belt and hastened to join his friend. "Olan! Junkie! Guys! When did you get back? How'd you find us out here?" With this exclamation, Saxon pulled a tall, lean man off his bike and crushed him into a bear hug. "Junkie!"

Junkie laughed, flipping his long, dark braid over his shoulder as Danjer grasped his hand. Leaving them together, Saxon dragged several more men from their bikes. "We rode into Judipeao a few hours ago," Junkie explained. "Evidently just missed you. Au'Banner pointed us in this direction."

"Took us a while to find you." Olan told them, patting the magnifoculars hanging around his neck.

"And once we found you, we had to watch for a while to make sure we had the right guys," Junkie cut in. "But I'd recognize your technique anywhere, Saxon," he conveyed with an evil smile. "Not to mention your remarkable ass. Haven't seen it since Geveena, but I recognized it."

"It's not my ass that's remarkable," Saxon shot back with a grin.

Olan pulled his timepiece out of his pocket, mournfully shaking his head as he gazed down at the small square on the end of the chain. The sun danced in his curling hair and glinted dully on a curl of embossed aluminum that decorated the shell of one ear. Olan shook his head. "There you are," he announced. "We haven't been here two minutes and he's already bragging about his equipment."

"Me? *Bragging*?" Saxon laughed as he waved a hand at Junkie. "I'm not the one with three stones announcing the fact that I have a dick!"

Junkie shrugged. "It isn't my fault you've only room for one cockstone."

"Mind you," Olan pointed out. "It *is* a *huge* one."

"Don't patronize the conceited bastard," Junkie argued. "Actually, from the little I saw—when I could wrestle the 'foculars off Olan—it was the girl who had the remarkable ass." He leaned sideways to put his eyes on Pink. "And I mean that in the nicest possible way," he announced solemnly, following these words with coarse laughter.

Pink caught Danjer's dark expression as his gaze cut to Saxon's face. Then Saxon was pulling her into his side, wrapping an arm around her protectively while he introduced her to the circle of men who belonged to Danjer's cavalry.

As soon as the introductions were completed, Junkie jerked his chin at the giant tick, wrecked on the ground a hundred feet away. "Did you guys bring the tick down?"

Saxon nodded. "It was trying to make a meal out of our imp," he explained.

Junkie's eyes fixed on Pink with a very contemplative and very male interest. "She's an imp?"

"That's not what he said," Danjer cut in with a disapproving growl.

Junkie tilted his head, questioning Danjer with an arched eyebrow.

"He said she's *our* imp."

Evidently intrigued by Danjer's response, Junkie nodded slightly without removing his gaze from Danjer's face.

"How was your break?" Saxon asked, filling in the silent gap.

"Good," Junkie answered. "We're ready to ride. How's your head?"

"Still there," Saxon told him with a laugh, running his hand back through his thick mane of tangled straw.

"That's more than can be said for the guy who hit you." Olan whistled. "Danjer waxed him."

Junkie nodded keenly. "Took him apart."

"What are friends for?" Danjer imparted with a malevolent smile while most of the men returned fierce grins of approval. Only one man looked a bit pale as he stared at the ground. Slightly smaller than the rest of the soldiers, the slender man also appeared to be younger than the others.

"Olan, Junkie and Scratch played with us before the war started," Saxon explained to Pink. "Everyone else, we met on the circuit. Camp and Blair used to be with Pumping Iron. Jake," he said, indicating the pale young man, "played with Once Burned. We lost a lot of guys at D'Almiers," he finished, his voice suddenly quiet and his gaze somber as he appeared to search the circle of men for fallen comrades.

"Once Burned?" Pink interrupted to change the subject. "You mean the band, Once Burned?"

"Yeah!" Saxon nodded. "The band. We were musicians before the war started."

Pink shook her head in uncertain disbelief as she stared around at the men, none of whom was without either a long sword or short axe.

"Everyone needs a peacetime profession," he told her as he backed away then turned toward his bike. "Just a minute. I'll show you." Saxon strode over to his bike, opened a saddlecase and lifted out three pieces of hardware, which he slotted together.

"You have your *keytar*?" Olan stated in open-mouthed awe. "You chopped your keytar and brought it back with you?"

Saxon shrugged. "It was Danjer's idea."

"But what about sound?"

Clipping the instrument onto his belt, Saxon adjusted the microphone in the neck of the keytar and cut a smiling glance at his bike. "Got that covered."

"No," Olan stated. "No. You *don't* have a sound system built into your bike."

"Just a small one," Saxon grinned, then fingered a series of keys while music exploded out of a speaker on the side of his saddlecase.

"Just a small one?" Junkie shouted.

"Well, the sound system's small. Danjer scavenged the card out of a handheld communicator." Saxon grinned. "But I didn't say anything about the speakers." With this explanation, Saxon jerked his chin at his friend. "Get your tambour, Danjer," he suggested. Moments later, Danjer stood beside him, slapping the Earther instrument against his muscular thigh, leaning his face close to Saxon's as they shared the mike positioned on the neck of the keytar. Danjer's hard, curving mouth was inches from Saxon's as his voice took the main melody and Saxon harmonized.

More than a little awestruck, Pink watched as Saxon's hands moved rapidly along the length of the long, slim instrument, pushing keys, adjusting sliders, bringing in violins along with a background of lutes, then drawing in a deep, exciting rush of bass drums and feathered cymbals. Frowning in concentration, he got the guitars arranged then the two friends shared a grin as Saxon joined Danjer again in the chorus.

"I can't believe you remember how to play," Junkie goaded Saxon when they had finished the song.

"There's nothing wrong with my memory, per se," Saxon taunted back as he unclipped the instrument from his belt. "I remember you chatting up that 'droid in Geveena."

Junkie hung his head then lifted it again with snap in his laughing eyes. "Hey! She was pretty," Junkie protested. "How was I supposed to know she was a 'droid?"

"Danjer knew."

"Yeah, well, Danjer could have told me before I—"

"Made an ass out of yourself?" Danjer suggested. "I have faith in you, Junkie. You'd have figured it out when you got her pants down."

Olan choked on a laugh. "Yeah. You'd have figured it out when you got her pants down—and discovered she had no working parts."

A rumble of hard male laughter swept the circle of men as everyone grinned at Junkie. "I don't know how you're supposed to tell them apart," Junkie grumbled, grinning at the same time. "How is it that you always know, Danjer?"

"Their skin tones are too gray," Danjer explained shortly.

"Skin tones?" Junkie shrugged expansively as he laughed and shook his head at his friends. "May I?" he asked Saxon as he reached for the keytar.

Passing Saxon's keytar around with careful reverence, the men took turns on it, handling the sleek instrument as they would a beautiful woman, dragging worshipping fingers down its long, polished length.

When it became clear that the impromptu jam session was going to last a while, they moved back to within two hundred feet of the tallicwood grove. Three of them ran back into town and returned with Shofu food and three cases of lemonale while the others dug up some groundwood and built a fire inside the circle of their bikes. The men sprawled on their bikes, their legs spread, their cockstones sparkling in the glow of the snapping fire as the afternoon sun paced across the sky. Junkie grinned at Pink when he caught her staring at the three flat pieces of webbed agate that made a triangle at the base of his fly.

Danjer took a turn on the keytar when it came his way. The dark Earther was easily as talented as Saxon. Wild and energetic, the music he created was as exotic as the planet from which he hailed. But, by far, the most accomplished musician was Jake, the slender man who had paled earlier when the men had been talking about Saxon's injury—and Danjer's revenge. He could keep a dozen instruments going at once— with unexpected flairs of brilliance—fifes where you least expected them, cellos taking the main melody. What he could do with the drums was pure genius.

They did some of their old songs then some of their newer songs then everybody's songs until the sun dipped behind the mountains and the evening deteriorated into songs about sex. A dry storm swept through without offering up a drop of moisture. They watched the lightning bang around in the nearby tallicwood trees as they emptied three cases of lemonale while sprawled a safe distance from the natural lightning rods.

With his instrument back in his hands, Saxon keyed a few bars and smiled. "One more," he told the group, starting into a slow melody.

The men groaned. "Not a fucking love song," they complained.

"One of the ladies in the audience requested it," Saxon said quietly, his gaze fixed on Pink's face. "Danjer?" he prompted, but the dark man shook his head with a cursory smile. The look Saxon gave his friend was one of reproach. "Well, it's Danjer's song," he spoke, "but I'll see if I can pull it off."

At the end of the song, the circle was silent as Pink stared from Saxon to Danjer. "You wrote that?" she asked incredulously. "You wrote 'A Love to Die For'?"

"You've heard it," Saxon stated.

"*Everyone's* heard it. Hard and Fast sang it."

"That's right. That's us. Danjer and me, Olan, Junkie and Scratch. Junkie and Danjer write most of our stuff. But the music's mine on that one," Saxon told her as he got to his feet. "The rest of the song is Danjer's." Pulling his keytar apart, he opened a saddlecase on the side of his bike. Pink joined him, passing Danjer, who was carrying their bedrolls to the far side of the fire.

"Danjer wrote the words to that song?" Pink asked Saxon as she watched him stow his keytar. She couldn't help the next question. "Who'd he write it for?"

"Who'd he write it for?" Saxon lifted an eyebrow as he smiled down on her. "You're not...what's the word?"

"Jealous?"

"You're not jealous, are you?"

"Should I be?" she blustered and blushed at the same time.

Slotting the three pieces of his instrument into their protective cases, he got them put away. "Maybe," he teased. "He wrote them for a great lady."

Pink's heart took a painful leap, her thoughts flying immediately to the duke's wife. "Great lady? How great? Would I have heard of her?"

"Oh, you've heard of her," Saxon laughed. He closed his saddlecase, then put an arm around her shoulders as he steered her back toward the fire. "Danjer," he called out as Pink scowled up at him. She wanted to stomp on his foot and shut him up before he could embarrass her in front of Danjer. "The imp here wants to know who you wrote that song for."

Danjer grunted from the darkness beyond the fire. "So why didn't you tell her?"

"I did! I told her you wrote it for a great lady."

"That's right," he called back. "I wrote it for the golden lady. I wrote it for money, Pink."

"Money?"

"Every band needs a love song if they hope to make it big," he announced loudly. "'A Love to Die For' was our big love song. Unfortunately, it hit the soundnet just before the war started and people were too distracted to listen to music. Then the net went out." He shrugged. "Saxon sings it. I can't do it with...the right emotion."

"You can't do it with a straight face," Saxon corrected him unkindly, grinning down at Pink.

Shrugging outwardly, Danjer nodded inwardly as he strode from the fire. Men wrote love songs for women — for women to buy. If women thought they represented anything real, they were deluding themselves. It was just fortunate for musicians that women were such hopeless romantics. Women fueled at least half of the sales on the soundnet.

Turning his head, Danjer's gaze stole back toward the fire where Saxon stood with his arm around Pink's shoulders. As he frowned across the space that separated him from the imp, an uncomfortable twinge possessed him. It was a mixture of longing and resentment and…something else.

Something he didn't believe in.

Shaking off the unwelcome emotion, Danjer selected a private location in a loose gaggle of infant tallicwood. As he stooped to roll out his bedding, a shadow moved nearby in the darkness. He looked up, his hand on his hilt. "Scratch?" he queried with a curious smile.

"Let me know when you guys turn in," Scratch said, his pupils huge and black, his gaze fixed on the fire where Pink stood in the curve of Saxon's arm. "I wanna be third man in. I've never fucked an imp before."

Slowly, stiffly, Danjer rose to stand beside him, his body drawing into a tight, battle-ready line.

"What?" Scratch laughed. "Did I say something wrong? You and Saxon are both fucking her, aren't you?"

"It's not like that," Danjer said in a tight rasp.

"No? What's it like, then?" he continued with a cocky smirk, missing the explosion brewing in Danjer's eyes.

Slowly, Danjer reached an arm out and laid it across the man's back, drawing him stiffly against his side. "It's like this," he said in a quiet voice of menace. "You touch the girl and I cut your balls off, as well as your dick. Then I give them to Saxon and he stuffs them down your throat."

"Oh." Scratch swallowed with a hard gulp. "It's like that, then, is it?"

Danjer gave him a very dark look. "Yes. It's like that."

"I'm s-sorry, Danjer," he stammered. "I didn't know. I-I was just thinking…that time in Geveena…when we all— I didn't mean to offend."

"I know," Danjer answered. "And that's the only reason you're not a eunuch right now, peeing out of a stump. Do me a favor," he added in a quiet voice of steel. "And make sure everybody else knows. I don't want to have to explain it twelve separate times."

Scratch gave him a wary smile. "Sorry," he repeated ruefully. "I'll tell everyone." His expression lightened. "I'll tell Junkie twice."

"Good idea," Danjer muttered darkly.

Fighting back a murderous urge to tear Scratch's head off, Danjer gave the man a shove to start him back toward the fire.

It was hardly Scratch's fault. It was an honest enough mistake. In the years they'd spent touring together, Danjer had never given Scratch any reason to expect anything different. Scratch had seen him with a lot of women, none of whom he valued over his bike or his sword…or his tambour for that matter.

But that didn't make Scratch's proposition any less annoying.

Blowing out a growling sigh, Danjer ripped his wrap over his head and threw it at the bedding. "Saxon," he shouted irritably, then watched with grudging satisfaction as Saxon steered Pink away from the fire. Stripping his leathers down his legs, Danjer stepped out of his pants then took Pink from Saxon, quickly undressing her while Saxon got rid of his own clothing.

"Does Junkie do…drugs?" Pink asked a little later when the three of them were lying naked together, sliding restlessly against one another. Pink was on her back and both men had their hands on her, stroking her smooth, nude flesh.

"Junkie?" Pink's question seemed to take a long time to get to Saxon's brain. "No," Saxon answered slowly. "Junkie docs women."

"What do you mean?"

"Junkie does women. He's addicted to women."

"He's addicted to sex," Danjer corrected Saxon with a harsh breath. Lying on his side, Danjer had his fingers wrapped around one of her breasts, cupping the luscious weight in his hand, rubbing his thumb over the pebbled surface of her nipple, appreciating its cheeky response as it stiffened beneath his touch. He nudged his lips into her hairline and swirled the rough tip of his wet tongue over her closest feeler. Her nubbin's reaction was remarkably similar to that of her puckering nipple. Like a delicate little piston wrapped in smooth nylon, the sluttish little nub surged into his mouth.

Pink caught up a quick breath. "No no no no no no no," she chanted softly. When she tried to pull her head away, Danjer followed her with his mouth. "Oh, oh, oh. Gently," she implored.

"Saxon," he murmured.

Saxon's mouth moved to her other feeler and together they suckled the tiny teat-like protrusions. Almost immediately, her hips started rolling to match the suction they applied to her nubbins.

Danjer laughed breathlessly as he lifted his gaze to watch her pelvis prod at the air. Saxon did the same. "Oh...now that's just sweet," Saxon whispered against her nubbin. "Did you ever see anything so sexy?"

Danjer shook his head in the darkness. "Does that feel good, Pink?"

She moaned. "You have no idea," she sobbed out in four agonized breaths. "Those things are pumping endorphins into my brain like there's no tomorrow."

"Yeah?" Saxon drawled in a low, lust-roughened voice, "and what are they pumping into your hips?"

"Erogenomorphins would be my guess," Pink moaned back at him.

"Erogeno—"

"She just made that up," Danjer murmured against her nubbin.

Danjer slid his hand down over her flat stomach, delaying to thumb the jewel in her belly before sliding lower to furrow a finger through the curls on her mound. Prodding a single finger into the top of her cleft, he watched her ride his finger for as long as he could stand it. His cock felt like it was ready to split, he was so fucking tight and hard. His knuckles brushed up against Saxon's as the blond's hand encroached between her thighs. With a growled obscenity, he fought the urge to warn Saxon off.

Pulling her away from his friend, Danjer lifted Pink's hips and turned her on her side, fitting her curving bottom into his groin. With his thick hot flesh dragging against her cheeks, he rubbed his fragile skin into her crease. In response, she rolled her hips to rub her ass against the press of his cock.

"Saxon," he breathed out.

"I've got it," Saxon answered. The sound of crisp paper rustled in the darkness as Saxon unwrapped the desiccating sticks. "Open her for me."

Danjer was already pulling her knee up over his thigh. Grasping at the sensitive flesh of her inner thigh, he spread her wide. "Will one stick be enough, Pink?"

She shook her head in the darkness. "Two would be safest," she offered in a shy voice. "Imps have children in pairs."

"Twins?"

"No, pairs. Two children. One for each of her male lovers. In separate wombs."

"Two, then," Danjer grunted, thinking of a dark child with a black mop of hair, playing alongside a fair child with green eyes. With an impatient flick of his head, he blinked the idea away.

Stretched over Danjer's body, Pink jumped when the narrow sticks prodded at the tender opening of her vagina. "Relax," Danjer whispered against her ear as Saxon slid the sticks home. Danjer groaned. "We're going to need a lot more sticks," he told his friend in a painful, panting laugh.

"You're telling me," Saxon grunted breathlessly.

Hard as a stake, Danjer entered her with a driving push. When she opened her mouth to scream, he reached up between her breasts and clamped his palm across the moist opening of her mouth. It a fit of sexual madness, she writhed and twisted, shafted on his cock. Her lips were wet and his palm slid over her mouth as he tightened his fingers to muffle the cries and shouts that fought to surface on her lips.

"Wait for me," Saxon complained in a harsh rasp.

"Get in there," Danjer berated him, sucking in a breath.

When Saxon pushed into her, she settled a bit, her moans softer and heavy with pleasure as both men fought for her, fought to slake their lust on her, fought to find pleasure and release inside the slick fire of her warm, willing cunt. Saxon's hands cased her waist while Danjer's fingers bit at her hip as they both thrust at her, their penises filling her, their cocks rubbing the length of each other while they pumped into her — each man trying to lead the drive and claim command.

In the midst of this struggle for dominance, Pink came, her cunt clamping down on the two thick cocks filling her vagina. Her teeth sank into Danjer's fingers, biting down hard as her head tossed. He tightened his grip to muffle her helpless sobs beneath his palm.

As her sheath tightened in a series of clenching spasms, Danjer's cock was forced against Saxon's inside the steamy noose of her channel. For several delicious seconds, movement was almost impossible as Pink's cunt strangled them pitilessly. Danjer's tip was caught beneath the rim of Saxon's crown. Clenching his teeth, he jerked his hips upward and rode up over Saxon's cock head as Saxon yelped in surprise. Danjer felt Saxon's testicles, hot and damp and suddenly rock-hard against his own.

As soon as Pink loosened a fraction, Saxon started moving. The pleasure was almost unbearable. The savage jerk of Saxon's hips and the brutal drag of Saxon's cock against his own thick shaft were darkly arousing in a way that Danjer didn't want to think about. He was having a hard enough time getting used to the idea of sharing the imp with another man, without having to deal with the idea of sharing an orgasm.

Viciously, Danjer pulled his hips as he slammed into the paradise between Pink's legs.

"I'm...coming," Saxon grunted harshly as he banged deep inside her. "You with me?"

"I'm there," Danjer gritted out as his cock head dragged up Saxon's length a final time and Saxon shouted with pleasure—coughing out an obscene assortment of hard words invoking Pink's name as well as Danjer's. Danjer felt Saxon's hot liquid cum erupt to coat his flesh like burning lava as he drove all the way in to pound against Pink's limit and ejaculate just behind his friend.

Danjer's neck curved inward and he buried his lips in Pink's neck to mute his next words—to stop himself from crying her name. "Jeezis," he moaned as he dragged his wet hand from her damp mouth and used his fingers to cup her breast. His dick was still inside her, loose but pulsing against Saxon's thick, used flesh. "Saxon," he groaned damningly. "You made enough noise to wake the dead."

They heard Junkie's laughter from afar. "We aren't *dead*, Danjer. We aren't asleep either," he added in a complaining laugh.

There were a few instants' silence, then Danjer's, "Shut up, Junkie."

"It's a bit too hard for sleeping," Junkie called back. "The ground," he added as an afterthought. "Not to mention everything else."

"Don't tell *me* your problems," Danjer growled in answer. "Cock it and pull it, Junkie." Grinning into the darkness, Danjer raised himself on one elbow as he gazed back to the fire where the other men were camped.

There was a rustle of sound as Junkie got to his feet and straightened beside his bike. "Think I'll have to, Danjer," he announced.

Danjer grinned as Junkie spread his legs and pulled out the long weight of his penis. Junkie's flesh glowed in the firelight as he dragged his fist down his cock several times and emptied onto the ground in several splashing spurts. Muttered groans followed, along with the sound of more men leaving their bikes and their beds. With a smug, satisfied smile warming him, Danjer dropped back down to the ground and snugged himself up against Pink.

"I'll take first watch," Saxon offered as he threw a glance at the fire and the men camped around it. "Short watches tonight? There's plenty of us to share them."

Danjer shook his head. "There's still a war going on. And the baroness is still looking for the imp. The only man I trust besides you is me."

"You don't trust the guys?" Saxon asked with a yawn and Danjer felt Saxon's thick flesh slide along his own as he pulled his slack penis from Pink's wet hold.

"Not even the guys," Danjer told him as Saxon pulled his leathers up his legs and ambled off toward the fire. With his arms wrapped around Pink, Danjer pressed a private kiss into her neck before he gave himself over to a few hours' sleep.

Chapter Ten

ഔ

Danjer was awake and on watch when the rest of the camp finally got up with the sun. After a quick breakfast of dried energy sticks and leftover Shofu, the party set out for the duke's palace in Judipeao. Danjer's men followed him to rejoin his ranks of cavalry at the Iron Palace.

The two days that followed were exceptionally fulfilling for Danjer—as well as darkly frustrating. He spent each night and a good part of each morning in the small bedroom with Pink and Saxon. Even though Saxon deferred to Danjer's need to dominate where sexual matters were concerned, somehow it still wasn't enough.

Danjer wanted more.

On the third morning back at the palace, Danjer woke in the small, closed room that the Duke had made Pink's bedroom. Judging by the amount of light filtering under the bedroom door, it was well past dawn. Stretching as he woke, he was surprised to find Pink's head on his chest, her arm flung around his waist as she slept. Saxon usually claimed her through the night, wrapped around her like she was the first and last thing he thought of. Wondering at this bit of luck, Danjer shifted as he looked across the large bed for the big blond. But Saxon was absent.

His stirring had wakened Pink and she moved against him in a long, languorous wave of smooth, slender limbs. Immediately, his morning hard-on throbbed with passionate interest and he rolled his body halfway over hers as he rubbed a kiss into her warm, sleepy mouth. Without opening her eyes, she wrapped her arms around his neck, responding to his kiss with a sweet, inviting readiness that gripped his lungs and crimped the edges of his heart. For several seconds, he forgot to breathe as his blood thickened in his cock. His heart expanded with a pang as he wondered if Pink even knew who kissed her—Saxon or himself.

He wondered if she cared.

"Danjer," she murmured against his lips, answering his question as though she'd read his mind. In that instant, he was almost overwhelmed with tenderness for the woman beneath him. Unexplainably proud and pleased beyond reason, he felt his dick knot and stretch against her sleek thigh.

The kiss he continued to press into her moist, open mouth seemed somehow illicit in Saxon's absence. As though he were stealing this preciously private moment. As though he were partaking of something forbidden or at least denied. As his breath thickened and his blood began to pound uncomfortably in his groin, he wondered how many more minutes or seconds he could steal with her before Saxon returned to the room.

He wanted her. He wanted her all to himself.

It would have to be quick.

Rolling off her, he turned Pink onto her stomach and pulled her hips up to put her on her knees. Her bottom rose into the air provocatively as he knelt behind her, swiftly moving between her legs, taking a brief moment to appreciate the naughty tilt of her ass as it thrust into the air.

He smoothed his hands over her heart-shaped bottom, as his eyes took in the spread of her rounded cheeks. Her legs were parted enough to expose the tight puckered kiss nestled in the cleft of her ass and the heavy pout of her pussy below. Her sexy lips were thick and deeply pink, enclosing the deep red heart of her hourglass opening. Her pussy breathed out her irresistibly tempting scent and he fought the urge to lower his mouth to the tender lips of her sex.

She'd been ridden brutally the night before, once as they'd retired then again in the middle of the night when both men had reached for her restlessly. Together they'd grappled in the dark—twisting and groping in a tangle of sweat-sheened limbs, wet cocks, sodden balls and sex-scented sheets as Pink screamed and thrashed, trapped between the hard press of their bodies.

But the nights and the mornings and the sex were always shared with Saxon. Today he would take her alone, if he could.

Reaching across the rumpled sheets, he searched through a small pile of discarded packages and empty papers until he came up with two unused desiccating sticks. Tearing at them with his teeth, he shook out their contents into his hand and pushed two of the transparent sticks into Pink's double vagina. He palmed her long opening, collecting some of her dewy moisture on his hand before he spread his knees to push her legs wider.

With her face buried in the pillows at her head, she murmured his name again. He wanted to respond. He wanted to answer with her name and more, but instead he notched into her and drove forward.

Immediately she reacted like a live wire, jumping insanely as he knelt behind her. With the blunt tip of his cock seated firmly at the back of her cunt, he held her firmly into his groin. Closing his eyes, he allowed himself a few seconds of pure blissful pleasure as she danced like a mad toy at the end of his dick.

"D-D-Danjer," she ground out in a stammer. "D-D-Danjer. H-h-help."

"I've got you," he murmured. "I've got you, Pink." He opened his eyes to watch her jolting backside. "I'll get you fucked, sweetheart. Just hold on."

For several moments longer he delayed, trapped in carnal pleasure as the walls of her vagina bore down on his shaft. He watched her tight little rosebud clench as her vagina sucked on his cock and he reveled in the crushing grip of her spasming cunt. Then, with a glance behind him at the bedroom door, Danjer acted. With his cock buried in the top of her hourglass opening, he reached down between his groin and her bottom. Swiftly, he plunged two fingers into the lower section of her vagina, cupping his balls in his wet hand as he rubbed his fingers along his shaft inside her. "Here you go, sweetheart."

She made several sobbing, choking noises and he felt her vagina clamp viciously along the length of his cock at the same time it rippled around his long fingers. She was coming and he rushed to join her, giving her a few short, sharp savage jabs as he rolled his balls in his wet palm. Clenching his teeth, he experienced a few instants of blank, noiseless, overwhelming ecstasy—empty of every sensation and sound but for the pleasure rooted at the base of his cock. Then he shot into her, filling her with his hot spend in a long steady surge that emptied his soul and drained him to the bottom of his heart.

Awed, he stared down on her back. He blinked at her smooth, firm ass cozied up to his groin in a warm kiss of flesh on flesh. Pulling back, he eased his cock free of her cunt as he leaned over to kiss her bottom and smooth her skin beneath his hand. Feeling both exhilarated and smug, he panted, flushed with pleasure and satisfaction—supremely satisfied to know that he didn't need Saxon to bring the imp to climax.

And *she* didn't need *Saxon*.

The next words startled him because they were Saxon's.

"Would you two stop that for a minute?"

Turning on his knees, Danjer squinted across the room to where Saxon stood just inside the door. His euphoria bled off in simple degrees as Saxon closed the door behind him. Staring at Saxon, Danjer wasted about two seconds wondering how long he'd been standing there before he realized Saxon must have opened the door as he was climaxing. It was the only way Danjer could have missed the sound of the door opening as well as the spill of light into the room.

Which meant that Saxon knew what he now knew.

Pink didn't absolutely require two lovers.

Saxon touched a small round panel on the wall to activate the room's neon lighting before he sauntered toward them. Dropping to sit on the bed beside them, the blond grinned as he bounced a small square box in his hand then tossed it at Pink. "Open it," Saxon instructed her with a smug smile.

As Danjer moved from behind her to sprawl on the bed's soft, snowy comforter, Pink folded her knees beneath her and rolled into a sitting position. With a questioning look aimed at Saxon, she reached for the tiny box nestled among the lacy pillows. When she slid the lid off the box, she gasped at the ring inside. Staring up at Saxon, she then cut a swift glance back to Danjer's face.

Upstaged by his best friend, Danjer averted his eyes as he felt his mouth flatten into a brooding line of disapproval.

"It's absolutely beautiful, but I can't accept it," Pink told Saxon in an unbroken rush of words. "It's far too expensive."

Saxon laughed. "It's bought and paid for and has your name engraved on the inside of the band. I don't think the jeweler in Judipeao will be wanting to take it back. Of course you can accept it!"

Pink stared worriedly at the beautiful shining stone set in platinum as her gaze traveled again to Danjer.

"Take the ring, Pink," he grunted in a flat tone without looking at the fabulous bit of jewelry. "Saxon can afford it. I've been working on something for you myself," he lied quickly, then paused. "I would have given it to you *sooner* but I didn't want to *show up* my best friend." With these words, he cut an accusatory glare at Saxon while the man's smile turned a bit crestfallen.

With his lips turning downward, Saxon's gaze shifted uncertainly a few times then finally rested on Danjer's left hand, still wet with Pink's cum. "Don't forget to wash your hands," he told Danjer as he lifted his eyes to meet Danjer's gaze. "You don't want to accidentally bind yourself."

There were a few instants of shared animosity as Danjer challenged his friend with a solemn stare.

Saxon returned his gaze unflinchingly.

Saxon knew.

* * * * *

It wasn't until the following morning that Danjer came through with the gift he'd promised Pink. She suspected that he hadn't, in fact, been working on anything before that morning when he'd taken her alone—without Saxon. At any rate, he had disappeared for the rest of that day, leaving her to spend it with Saxon.

The kind-hearted warrior was good company and she enjoyed the long, relaxed hours she spent with him. At the same time, she missed Danjer's vitally energetic presence. While there was no doubt in her mind that she loved Saxon without reserve, she also recognized that Danjer was the man she was *in love* with.

Saxon made her melt. But Danjer made her burn.

When Danjer failed to show up for dinner, Saxon went looking for him and returned with a reassuring grin. "He'll be in soon," he told her. But when it got late, they almost fell asleep together, fully dressed and buried in the duke's deep, luxurious bedding, waiting for Danjer in Saxon's room. When Saxon kissed her, she stroked her hand up the long length of his thick erection then rubbed the heel of her palm into his groin. But he pulled her hand away. "We'll wait for Danjer," he told her and kissed her again, almost chastely this time.

She marked the difference between the two men. Danjer would never have missed an opportunity like this. In Saxon's absence, Danjer would have taken her in a heartbeat. But Saxon wouldn't take advantage of his friend's absence.

Unless she made him.

Pink was pretty sure that there were some things a man couldn't refuse.

She was concerned that Saxon might feel left out after what he had seen that morning — when he'd walked in to find her and Danjer coupling without him. She wanted Saxon to understand that he was just as important to her as was Danjer. In addition, she had a deep private interest in provoking the gentle giant. As a woman, she was intrigued by his implacability. She wanted to know if she could release the primitive passion she was certain he kept under wraps in Danjer's presence. Alone with him, she thought she might be able to unleash the aggressive side of his nature.

Undressing quickly, she stretched out beside him and rubbed up against him, pressing her breasts against his chest and snuggling her mound into his crotch.

He growled.

Reaching between their bodies, she stroked him a few times.

"Pink," he warned her.

"I'm not going to…I'm not going to…"

"No," he affirmed. "You're not." He blew out a sigh as he moved away from her just an inch or two. "But I guess it wouldn't hurt if you played a little bit…with my dick."

Immediately, she scooted down on his body as he rolled onto his back. It didn't take long for her to get him unfastened and work his huge, heavy shaft out of his pants. Ridged and wrapped in dark veins, his impressive erection looked good enough to eat. She rubbed her lips over the wide crown. The thin skin that covered his iron hard penis felt like the finest gossamer against her lips. She checked his face. His eyelids were half closed and the corners of his rugged lips curved lazily upward as he watched her lips on his cock.

As she played with his cock, his legs moved apart and his chest lifted in short, shallow waves. Sliding her hand lower, into his leathers, she fingered his testicles, collecting and recollecting the thick weight of his scrotum into her hold. His hips began to move fractionally, matching the rhythm with which she stroked him. With her cheek against his straining length, she rubbed her face into his cock then turned her lips and kissed him slowly all the way up his shaft. When she got to the top, she took his cock head in her mouth.

That was where Saxon drew the line.

Normally patient to the extreme, Saxon lost his composure faster than she would have thought possible. She was wrong about what she thought a man couldn't refuse. Saxon *could* refuse her advances. It wasn't easy for him though. And he had to tie her down to make sure he refused them.

Rolling away from her, he shoved his cock back inside his leathers before he disappeared into the slashroom.

Smiling guiltily, Pink tucked her legs beneath her, sitting up as she watched the slashroom door. There was a harsh sound of tearing cloth then Saxon emerged carrying the remnants of a dark towel in one hand.

She only had a chance to squeal before he had her by the ankle. He flipped her onto her belly then dragged her to the bottom of the bed where he spread her legs while she wriggled and protested and called him names—none of which helped in the least. By the time he finished with her, they were both laughing, but she was tied down. Firmly tied down.

Tearing more strips of soft terrycloth, Saxon knotted the short lengths around her ankles and fixed her feet to the styrowood floor with two crossbow bolts. Then he pushed the side of her face against the sheets and pulled her arms out to either side of the mattress. Her hands didn't reach the edges of the wide bed, so he'd been forced to use longer pieces of toweling, which he wrapped around her wrists and likewise bolted to the floor.

She didn't put up much of a fight. She figured Saxon was strong enough to have his way with her, should he be so inclined. Pleasantly enough for her, he looked pretty much inclined.

"This isn't very comfortable," she complained, laughing as he tied the final knot. It wasn't. Since her legs were so long, there was almost a foot of space between her stomach and the bed.

"I'm not done," he argued gruffly. Grabbing up several soft pillows, he stuffed them under her belly. "How's that?" he asked with an amused rumble, sounding pleased with himself.

She let loose a contented sigh. "That's better."

"Good," Saxon grunted. Then he dragged a chair across the room and threw himself into it. A mirror on the wall beside her allowed her to see most of Saxon as he sat behind her. In the following moments his pleased expression slowly evaporated, growing hungry and intense as he focused his gaze between her legs. Pulling his cock out of his leathers, he stroked his shaft as he watched her pussy.

She looked at her own reflection. Her normally pale pupils were almost entirely black. Her lips were slack as she panted softly.

Into this loaded silence intruded the jarring sound of the door opening. Pink's vagina tightened once in greedy anticipation. The first thing Danjer would see was her sex, spread and waiting for him. The door closed quickly. There were a few seconds of silence, then Danjer's voice. "What are you doing?"

"Waiting for you," Saxon growled from the chair. "And it hasn't been easy either."

Pink heard Danjer's cleats as he crossed the floor. She saw him in the mirror before he came into view beside the bed. Slowly, he lowered himself to sit beside her head, leaning away from her to slide something under a pillow at the top of the bed. Although she assumed this would be the gift he'd been working on, she wasn't able to catch a glimpse of it before it disappeared beneath the white pillowcase.

"Why is she tied down?" Danjer asked, his tone husky and low.

"Because she wouldn't leave me alone," Saxon answered.

Danjer smiled as he looked at her face, turned on the bed. "Have you been a naughty girl, Pink?"

"A little," she admitted with a restless giggle.

"And just look where it's gotten you."

"Yes," she panted cheerfully. "It worked, didn't it?"

"Did she put up much of a struggle?"

Saxon gave a low rumble of hard laughter. "Just enough to make it interesting."

"Interesting...or arousing?"

"Oh fuck," he snorted, "I was aroused before we got started."

Danjer reached out and tucked a pale strand of her hair behind her ear. "Did you try to fuck Saxon without me?" he asked in a silky voice that slid like a knife.

Pink only hesitated an instant. "I love Saxon," she told him bravely.

"I don't care if you love Saxon without me," he told her with a stern smile. "I just don't want you fucking him without me. You got that, Pink?"

"Saxon wouldn't let me," she argued. "Why do you think I'm tied down?"

"Because Saxon's a good friend. And *you're* a naughty girl." Languorously, he traced his finger around her jawline. "Are you comfortable, Pink?"

She wiggled her butt in the air. "Oh god yes, but..."

"But?"

"But I want you," she groaned. "I want you both. Only, I don't know how both of you are going to get on me."

"Don't worry," Danjer murmured. "We'll come up with something." He gazed across the room at Saxon. "How do you want to do this?"

"With both of you," Pink answered.

Danjer chuckled deeply. "I wasn't asking you," he told her.

She made a slight huffing sound wrapped up in a giggle. "Don't I get any say in the matter?"

"No," both men answered in unison.

"You're the one who got herself tied down," Danjer pointed out quietly as he stood and moved behind her. "So, how do you want to do this?" he asked Saxon again.

Saxon shifted his feet as he watched his thumb, the blunt digit pressed against the slit on his cock head. "With me standing behind her."

There was a long silent pause filled with Pink's soughing breaths.

"You underneath her," Saxon added firmly.

There was more silence. Apparently this arrangement didn't particularly appeal to Danjer.

"Hey," Pink panted as she squirmed. "If you guys can't agree on how to do this, I'll take it to the men's barracks. I'm sure they'll have some ideas."

"You won't be *taking it* anywhere," Danjer told her in a warning voice. "In fact, the only place you'll be *taking it* — is in the backside."

Pink giggled. "You're all talk, Danjer. All talk and no cock."

Danjer's hand connected with her bottom with a sharp smack of sound.

"Ouch! Saxon! Don't let him do that!"

"I'm sorry, Pink," Saxon drawled. "But that last comment *was* a bit...what's the word?"

"Provoking?" she suggested.

"No."

"Insulting," Danjer stated darkly.

"That's the word," Saxon agreed cheerfully.

"Insulting," Danjer repeated. "You'd think someone tied down with her ass in the air would be a little more...circumspect."

Pink snorted.

"She doesn't appear to be taking this very seriously," Danjer pointed out to Saxon. "Personally, I think we rate a little more respect."

Saxon shrugged. "I like her this way."

Pink felt Danjer's heat rolling off his body as he stood inches from her backside. "I like her this way too," he said in a whisper, his eyes on the parting between her cheeks. He ran a finger through her slot. "She's wet. What have you been doing to her?"

Saxon shook his head, his eyes following Danjer's finger up through her cunt. "Just watching her."

"Just watching her? She's awfully wet for 'just watching her'. What's up with that, Pink?"

"Hey," she breathed, "I'm easy."

"You got the sticks?" Danjer asked next.

"They're ready when you are," Saxon told him.

Danjer's hand smoothed over the heated skin where he'd spanked her. His fingers clenched on a warm handful of ass then loosened to stroke her flesh again. "*I'll* take her from behind," he challenged Saxon.

More silence.

Saxon cleared his throat. "I reckon I'm strong enough to tie you down too, Danjer."

"You *might* be able to," Danjer allowed in a dangerous voice, "if I didn't kill you, first."

"If you didn't kill me," Saxon agreed calmly.

"Well hell," Danjer finally said, "I guess when you put it that way..." Danjer returned to Pink's side, pulling off his wrap and unfastening his leathers. He pushed his pants and jockstrap down his dark, lean, muscular legs and stepped out of them. His viciously long cock swung in an arc as he moved toward her. Leaning over, he dropped a kiss on Pink's slack, wet mouth. After pulling the pillows out from beneath her, he wriggled in underneath her. As Danjer worked his way between her and the sheets, Pink could see Saxon in the mirror, throwing his clothes on the chair.

"Hello, beautiful," Danjer said from approximately two inches away. Wrapping a hand around her neck, he brought her mouth to his. She reacted immediately to the slide of his hot lips, moaning shamelessly as his tongue took her mouth. His legs were between hers, his knees bent and his feet on the floor. His warm, damp, all-male body was beneath hers and she smudged herself against him, absorbing his hard, ridged texture along the whole length of her torso. His cock was an imposing line of steel pressed into the length of her belly and reaching up into her midriff.

He felt good. He tasted good. And she was so ready for this—hungry and eager and full of agonizing heat. She rocked against him as his tongue probed between her lips and thrust deep inside her mouth.

Then she felt Saxon behind her, pulling her cheeks wide as he slotted two protective sticks against her double entrance, pressing them all the way in. Grasping her hips, he pulled her ass into his groin and rubbed his cock between her cheeks. His thighs were against hers, his feet braced just outside her feet. His steel-hard legs were moist with sweat. His groin was damp, his cock wet and probably streaming at the head as he dragged it through her crease. His voice was deep and strained when he asked, "Are you ready, Pink?"

Her answer was captured inside Danjer's mouth as his hand on her nape forced her to accept the rough intrusion of his tongue. "Mmm," she moaned, tangling her tongue with Danjer's and pushing her bottom back against Saxon.

"Put her on your cock, Danjer."

"Okay," Danjer panted, pulling his lips from the satin warmth of Pink's mouth. "But give me a few minutes inside her. I haven't just spent two hours alone with her. It's gonna take me a few seconds before I'm ready to come."

Sliding down her body, Danjer positioned his cock head against her entrance then shoved into her. Immediately, she started to orgasm, screaming and thrashing as much as her bindings would allow. Danjer sucked in a breath. "This shouldn't take long," he told Saxon.

"No," Saxon told him. "This *won't* take long."

Danjer almost choked when he felt Saxon's hands on his balls. "What are you doing?" He lifted his head so that he could glare over Pink's shoulder at the blond giant.

"Just making sure this doesn't take long," Saxon answered with an evil smile. With one big hand, he fingered Danjer's testes while he cupped his own balls in his other palm.

Danjer ground his teeth as Pink's cunt and Saxon's grasping touch propelled him toward climax at hyper speed. "Fuck," he ground out as Pink's hot channel throttled his dick and Saxon's touch teased him toward madness.

"You there?" Saxon asked him.

Danjer's hips began to jerk spasmodically.

"Close enough," Saxon laughed breathlessly just before he shafted Pink in one huge thrust.

Danjer shouted as Saxon's cock head rode up the long, entire length of his exploding shaft. "Damn you, Saxon. I'll fucking kill you. I'll fucking…"

Saxon's thick rod continued to ride Danjer's penis. When Saxon pulled back and slammed home, his testicles swung heavily to surge against Danjer's tight balls. As Danjer ejaculated in endlessly long surges, strangled roars of pleasure burst up the column of his throat. Then he felt everything squeeze tighter around his cock as Saxon expanded beside him. And everything got hot and wet and still and incredibly full as Saxon's dick pulsed against his own and the big man gritted his way through several choking obscenities.

Fucking hell.

"Saxon," Danjer muttered, "if you ever reach for me again, I swear it will be the last thing you ever do."

"I was just trying to help," Saxon imparted with a panting smirk.

"Bullshit! You were just helping yourself, you impatient bastard."

"What are you complaining for?" Saxon pointed out mildly. "It worked, didn't it?"

"*What am I*— When I need help fucking a woman, Saxon, I'll ask...for my last rites. You got that?"

"Yeah," he growled back like a gloriously sated tiger, "I got that, Danjer."

* * * * *

Pink fell asleep tucked into Saxon's side. When she woke, the large airy bedroom was filled with glorious morning light that arrowed through the windows. Danjer's long lean body, sprawled out beside her own, had replaced Saxon's huge frame. Resting on the pillow that lay between them, Danjer's gift gleamed in the slanting rays of the morning sun.

Pulling herself up and tucking her legs beneath her, Pink reached for the strange piece of hand-fashioned jewelry. Shaped like a thick torc with fat, looped ends, many strands of copper wire had been twisted into the shape of a plain open circlet. Along its circumference, hanging at equally spaced intervals, shone little square electrical connectors of the same material. The variously sized connectors had been carefully scored with radial sunbursts so that they caught and reflected the morning light that sloped through the windows. When Danjer stirred next to her, she quickly pushed the necklace onto her neck. Although it was thick, the thin stranded wire sat lightly on her collarbones.

The fact that Danjer had made it for her with his own hands made Pink's heart feel tight and full. Topped up with emotion, she watched his sleeping face, his black eyelashes edging his closed eyes, his dark hair fanned out on the white pillow beneath his head, his jaw shadowed with the black prickle of his overnight beard.

The dark warrior looked somehow out of place in the elegant palace bedroom. As though he didn't quite belong to comfortable bedrooms with soft white bedding and lacy pillows. Like a dark panther gliding through the gridded streets of an ordered city, Danjer looked like he belonged somewhere else. Danjer belonged to all things primal and elemental. He belonged to the forests and the plains and the endless sand wastes. He was too wild to be kept indoors.

The bedroom door opened and scuffing footsteps brought Saxon over to her. He put a cup of char in her hands as he grinned at the necklace. "He's really gone all out with that," Saxon teased in a quiet voice, lifting his chin at the sleeping man beside her.

She smiled at him uncertainly.

"He's emptied out his toolkit for you."

Her tentative smile unwound as her heart unraveled just the slightest bit.

"Don't look so disappointed," Saxon reassured her with laughing eyes. "He wouldn't have parted with the contents of his toolkit unless he planned to keep you. Think about it. What's he going to do for spare parts if he ever loses you?" Saxon sipped from his own steaming cup then pointed at the copper necklace around her neck. "For a guy like Danjer, that's like giving you the key to his house."

She nodded wryly.

"Too bad he doesn't have a house," Saxon added airily. "Just don't be surprised if he needs to borrow a connector back one day."

"Fuck you," Danjer growled sleepily, rubbing a thick wrist over his eyes before opening them. "If I need any spare parts, I'll steal them off your bike." Rolling up into a sitting position, Danjer smiled at Pink before he reached out and turned the torc on her neck, resettling it so that the open ends were positioned beneath her chin. "You wear it like this," he told her gently.

The door slammed open and Danjer pushed Pink behind him on the bed while Saxon leapt to his feet, sword in his fist. But it was the duke standing breathlessly in the open doorway, belting his sword around his waist. "She's moving," he shot at them in two words. "The baroness. Meeting in five minutes."

Chapter Eleven

ഔ

After a quick trip to the slashroom with Pink, Danjer dressed in record time. He led the way as the trio clattered down the stone stairs to join Au'Banner and the rest of his captains in the dining hall. The men and women moved restlessly, their weapons rustling against their leathers, their cleats thudding dully on the pliant, styrowood floor. Small wounds appeared on the soft surface of the floor, closing slowly with time.

Au'Banner caught Danjer's eye then placed himself at the head of the table while his officers hurried to sort themselves out and find chairs. Saxon pushed Pink ahead of him and installed her between himself and The Lady.

Chloe's previously feminine persona was stripped away, her flowing gown replaced with leather, her gilded sash changed out for a weapons belt snugged tight around her hips. Danjer grinned. The Lady looked good in a dress. But she looked even better with a sword on her hip.

For the sake of speed, Pink had pulled on one of The Lady's borrowed gowns, belting it around her waist as they'd left the bedroom. Now Danjer found his eyes drawn to the delicate folds draped over her shoulders and covering her breasts. The soft fabric was creamy white and, though the lack of color highlighted the pink in her cheeks, he longed to see her in something bright and bold like royal blue or deep crimson.

Au'Banner dropped into his chair and the room was instantly silent as the soldiers waited for the duke's report. "The baroness is on the move," he told them. "Aleya?"

A small attractive woman with closely cropped hair took up the discourse. "I got a radio communication twenty minutes ago from Farra. She reported the baroness opened her gates at 0500 this morning. A column of ten thousand emerged and turned north. My scouts set up a transmitter relay, staying just ahead of her. It was intact as of thirty minutes ago but, of course, they'll try to knock out our positions.

"The town of Marpena is besieged as of this moment," Aleya stated grimly.

"The garrison at Marpena can hold them off for a few hours, but we have to move," Au'Banner summarized. "I'll lead out with my personal guard. Danjer's cavalry will follow. Damen's mounted infantry behind him. Then Betta, Anton and Jason with their infantry units." The duke settled his gaze on Danjer. "Warn and Terra will stay behind with their companies to protect the palace, along with The Lady and her personal guard. The Lady will be in command here until my return." With these words, the duke stood as his captains strode from the room.

Danjer hesitated as his gaze went from Pink to Saxon. He didn't like the way this was shaping up. He'd expected the baroness to bypass the small city of Marpena and strike directly north when she finally made her move.

"I want both of you with me," the Duke ordered, cutting a pointed gaze at Danjer before he turned and paced through the doors. Still Danjer and Saxon lingered an instant, their gazes locked as they worried together. Danjer turned to The Lady. "This could simply be a diversionary tactic," he stated. "Planned by the baroness to get to Pink."

"I know that, Danjer," The Lady informed him crisply. "That's why Pink is staying here, rather than accompanying you to the front. That's why Au'Banner left two units behind rather than the one he'd normally leave to protect the palace. Let me do my job," she told him. "I've several years of experience on you." Her expression softened as she smiled sympathetically. "If you do your job, we'll never see the baroness's army."

Not entirely convinced and not in the least happy, Danjer gave The Lady a curt nod. As Saxon kissed Pink goodbye, Danjer stalked from the hall with his hand on the hilt of his sword.

* * * * *

"Au'Banner should have sent news by now," The Lady told Pink at the end of the day, unable to conceal the concern that tightened her voice. "There's nothing on the transmitter but that's not unusual. It's hard to keep a line of communication intact during a battle. Still, I'd have thought he'd get one of his men back to us by now." Frowning thoughtfully, The Lady peered through the great hall's windows into the darkening southern sky.

Standing beside her as Chloe paced, Pink shifted her feet restlessly. The hem of her gown stirred against the styrowood floor. The evening storms had run their course and had disappeared into the west.

Suddenly, Chloe turned her frown on Pink. "What are you going to do about Saxon and Danjer?" she asked.

"What do you mean?"

Chloe shrugged. "They're obviously both in love with you. How are you going to choose between them without destroying their friendship?"

Pink regarded her seriously. "I'm not going to choose. I need both of them."

"How does that work?"

"Imps are made for two lovers." She hesitated. "Physically, it works just fine."

Chloe appeared to digest this information. "And how does it work emotionally?"

Now it was Pink's turn to shrug but the action wasn't offhand so much as defensive.

"I don't see how it's going to work," Chloe persisted quietly. "Danjer is so...passionate."

"You mean dominant?" Pink said.

"If that's what you'd call it." Chloe hesitated. "I don't see how it's going to work because Saxon's not the type to be dominated. He's too...strong.

"Danjer has to lead. That's why he's a captain and Saxon isn't. Of course, since Saxon's injury, he probably couldn't command his own unit anymore. But even before he got hit, Saxon would rather fight alongside Danjer than take the lead. But Saxon is strong. Saxon's a fighter." Chloe paused. "The difference is that...Danjer's a killer."

Pink nodded. "Saxon is strong. I guess I'm counting on his strength to make it work. I'm counting on his strength to hold us together." She paused a moment, lost in her thoughts, before she lifted her gaze once more to The Lady.

"What was he like...before?" she asked.

"Saxon? Before his injury? Pretty much the same. A little more confident. A little more arrogant," Chloe laughed. "If you can imagine that."

Pink's lips curved into a small smile as she thought of a *more* arrogant Saxon. More questions about her lovers hovered on the tip of her tongue, but there was sudden shouting outside on the palace walls and the huge, ironclad gates swung open to admit a lone rider.

"Who's that?" The Lady murmured, her eyes on the window as she moved toward the door. "He's not one of my husband's men."

"It's Jake," Pink exclaimed, turning quickly to follow her. "One of Danjer's cavalry. One of his friends." Rushing from the hall and down the corridor, the two women hurried down the wide palace steps into the yard.

Jake's bike dropped to the ground and he staggered a few steps toward the women as they approached him. His leather jacket was slashed in several places. His face was dirty and creased with weary lines as he reached out and steadied himself with a hand on Pink's shoulder.

"I've come from Marpena," he croaked before The Lady had a chance to question him. "The b-baroness's army was turned back," he glanced at Pink's face, "at a heavy toll." He looked at The Lady next. "Au'Banner's on his way back, t-traveling slowly. There are a lot of wounded."

The Lady blew out a tense breath of relief. "Why didn't Au'Banner send one of his own men?"

Jake shook his head. "He didn't have one to spare. Saxon sent me ahead. He wouldn't l-leave Danjer."

Pink uttered a small cry as her hands flew to her mouth. The tense knots that had gripped her stomach all day boiled into ugly clumps of terror and for several seconds she thought she'd be sick.

Not Danjer. Oh please, not Danjer.

"He got hit...hard. They're bringing him back but...it's bad, My Lady."

"Take me to him," Pink said immediately, moving swiftly toward Jake's bike.

"I d-don't know, Pink," Jake shook his head as he hesitated. "Saxon will kill me if anything happens to you...too."

"That's right, Pink," Chloe spoke up swiftly. "Neither Danjer nor Saxon would want to risk your safety. You know that."

Pulling the gown's long skirt up to clear her knees, Pink straddled the bike. "Take me to him," she ordered, forcing the terror-ripped words out of her constricted throat, trying desperately to sound both strong and uncompromising. "Now."

Jake waited for The Lady's command.

Pink's eyes narrowed on Chloe. "You'd go if it were Au'Banner," Pink stated and The Lady gave her a tight nod.

Jake shrugged at The Lady apologetically. "The road is safe enough between here and the return line," he offered. "They're only about an hour behind me."

The Lady glared at him, biting her lip as she considered Pink's determined expression.

Jake took a step closer to the duke's wife. "I d-don't think he'll make it back," Jake told her quietly. "If we're going, we need to leave now."

* * * * *

Several hours later, Danjer was the first man through the duke's ironclad gates, Saxon at his side as the laughing men dismounted. A column of bikes followed the forerunners into the palace yard, the beams from their headlights spearing ahead like ghostly javelins. The duke's army pulled into the yard in orderly units, guiding their bikes into the recharge slots as they parked in neat rows.

Throwing a leg over the back of his bike, Danjer punched a button. His vehicle settled to the ground as the headlight winked out. With Saxon's arm across his shoulders and his armored helm under his arm, they veered off to join the Duke before heading for the palace.

But the Duke was frowning across the yard at his wife, who was jogging toward them. The courtyard was lit on all sides and four shadows leapt at her feet like black petals ravaged by a dark wind. "Something's wrong," Au'Banner muttered.

Danjer's stomach knotted as he took in Chloe's expression. Apprehensively, he scanned the lighted yard for Pink.

"I let him take Pink," Chloe reported breathlessly, stopping abruptly just before she reached the men, gaping at Danjer and skimming his limbs with her eyes. "Banner! I let him take Pink. Jake—Danjer's friend. He rode in here three hours ago, reporting that Danjer was...mortally wounded. Pink insisted on going with him to meet the return column. By the Princess! We thought he was taking her to *you!*"

The Duke moved immediately toward his wife, pulling the distressed woman into his arms. "It's all right," he told her. "We'll get her back."

She shook him off, her expression one of absolute mortification. "I'm sorry, Danjer."

It took Danjer a second to gather his wits. "Jake volunteered to ride for the palace when it was clear we had the battle in hand. We let him take the message rather than send one of Au'Banner's regulars—to get him out of the fight because Jake is...Jake is...

"Why would he do that?" he asked abruptly, turning to his best friend for help, searching Saxon's face as he voiced the question. "Why would Jake take Pink?"

Saxon looked panicked as well as guilty. "He's taking her to the baroness."

Danjer shook his head in bewilderment. "How would he...how would he even *know* about the baroness?"

Saxon stared back at Danjer miserably. "Because I told him," he said in a low voice. "I told everybody about Pink and the baroness that night around the fire. It was *the guys*," Saxon tried to explain.

Without a word, Danjer turned and strode for his bike.

"Fuck!" Saxon exploded, ripping his hands through his hair as though he wished he could tear his head off. He took a moment to give The Lady a painful frown of sympathy. "It's not your fault," he told her as he backed away from her. "We'll bring her back."

"We'll recharge and turn around as fast as we can," the duke called to him. "We'll be right behind you!"

Saxon acknowledged this with a jerk of his chin then turned to race for his bike. Together, the two men sped through the gates as Au'Banner's army continued to funnel into the yard.

* * * * *

As dawn crept over the land and spilled a little pale light across the sand wastes southeast of Judipeao, Danjer stared angrily at the ground. In the sandy soil at his feet, he could clearly make out the trail of a single bike diverging from the paved road and heading south across the open land. "He's taking her to the baroness," Danjer stated flatly. Lifting his head, he glared straight ahead, south along the route that would take them to the baroness's palace.

Beside him, Saxon straddled his bike. "He didn't stay on the road to Marpena?" Saxon asked with faltering hope.

Danjer shook his head, then exploded. "Damn Jake! What was he thinking? I'd break his scrawny neck if he wasn't so fucking pathetic."

"Jake's always been—"

"A coward," Danjer shouted. "He's always been a fucking coward! What were you thinking, telling everyone about Pink? There's nothing more dangerous than a guy like that."

"Okay!" Saxon roared back with sudden fury. "All right! I fucked up. But Jake's not a coward. He's just afraid. He's always been afraid. *You* try spending your whole life getting beat on and see how *you* turn out," he yelled. "At least you had parents who loved you."

"Fucking O," Danjer screamed at the sky. "Don't make me feel sorry for the little bastard."

"He should never have been drafted," Saxon argued pointlessly. "Guys like that shouldn't be sent to war. He won't hurt Pink," Saxon finished with a dark, defensive grunt.

Danjer stared at his friend in disbelief. Then his voice cut the air like a knife. "He'd *better not* hurt Pink, Saxon. Because, let me tell you, if I find she's been harmed—*in any way, whatsoever*—Jake's not going to be afraid anymore. Because Jake's not going to be *alive* anymore!"

"She'll be okay, Danjer."

"Maybe. But Jake can tell the baroness he's seen her orgasm. After that, they'll be sticking all sorts of things in her. And they won't be glass *or* rubber!" Shoving off, Danjer glided away from Saxon.

"Is this the way south?" Saxon called, turning his bike to follow him.

Danjer shook his head. "We're going to Marpena first. There's a junk shop on this side of the city," Danjer told him without looking back. "I want to hit it before we head south."

Saxon glanced at the timepiece set into his handlebar. "It'll still be closed when we get there," he ventured apprehensively.

"Then we'll open it," Danjer told him with determination. "We'll need a few bits and pieces if we're going to pull off those modifications we talked about making to your bike."

Chapter Twelve

ഔ

Danjer squinted into the early morning sun as he stood with Saxon in the middle of the baroness's courtyard. Two crossbows were trained on them as Danjer carefully unclasped his weapons belt, refastened it and let it drop to hang on the handlebar of his bike. At his side, Saxon did the same.

Slowly, casually, Danjer raised his hands into the air. "We're musicians," he announced with his hands lifted above his head. "We followed our girlfriend here. She's an imp. Have you seen her? Light hair? Pale eyes?"

"Long legs?" Saxon added with a suggestive drawl and a keen smile.

When the bowmen lifted their crossbows a notch and sighted down along the length of their weapons, Danjer changed tack. "We're here to entertain the baroness. Before you kill us, I suggest you let her know that two members of Hard and Fast are in the courtyard."

Fifteen minutes later they were led from their bikes, their wrists manacled at their backs as two bowmen and two more guards accompanied them through the palace doors, down a wide corridor and into the great hall.

"Nice spread," Saxon pointed out with a grunt, craning his neck to take in the huge windows that ran from the polished styrowood floors to the high vaulted ceilings of the circular hall. "Hasn't changed much since we played here…three years ago?"

"More like four," Danjer answered.

"That was when the Copper Duke was still alive," Saxon reminisced quietly. "Before the baroness started her advance on the North." He sighed, shaking his head. "For a few months we had it made. Our musical careers were about to take off. Then the war started. What a frickin' troublemaker that woman is!"

The baroness's men chained them to one of the huge tallicwood posts that supported the vaulted roof. With their electric batons drawn and flickering a blue fire, the two guards stepped back to join the bowmen. There, the soldiers guarded their captives from a safe distance. Saxon and Danjer now found themselves with their arms wrapped partway around the post's wide diameter, their wrists shackled behind the thick pole.

After a long wait, Saxon slid to the floor, one knee bent as his booted foot rested on the styrowood floor, his other long leg sprawled out on the floor's gleaming surface.

Danjer remained on his feet, slouching against the sleek, metallic surface of the wooden post. Quietly tense, he worried about Pink and wondered where the fuck the baroness was.

He wasn't going to stand there against that post forever.

Finally, the doors cracked open and two burly guards shoved into the room, pushing the doors wide, ahead of the baroness's entourage. The baroness was preceded by her small personal guard of four and followed by her attendants. The doors remained open as several members of her court filtered in behind her procession.

The baroness's many gold necklaces rustled metallically as she glided across the hall and made her way to a raised dais on the opposite side of the room. A double train of heavy black and gold brocade trailed her as she swept like a wasp across the room. A black leotard accentuated the supple curves of her hourglass torso and a turban of cloth-o-gold wrapped her head, hiding her hair.

The baroness was a looker, although Danjer didn't much care for the black lipstick she had plastered on her lips.

Arranging herself regally on her throne, the elegant aristocrat crossed her long, freckled legs and tilted her head as she silently regarded the chained men.

"We've come for our imp," Saxon announced without preamble from his place on the floor. Tossing his head, he flicked his tangled hair of out his eyes.

The baroness seemed amused rather than offended by Saxon's boldness. "Who are you?" she asked calmly.

"We're musicians," Danjer took up. "The imp is our girlfriend. We want her back."

"You don't look like musicians," the baroness drawled, eyeing their cleated boots with a daintily arched brow. "You look like soldiers."

Saxon shifted his legs on the polished floor and frowned at his boots for a short, thoughtful instant. "Part of the act," he explained to the baroness with a satyr's grin. "The cleats are sexy. The girls love them."

The baroness gave him a wry, one-sided smile. "What makes you think your girlfriend is here?"

"She left with one of our friends," Danjer answered. "We tracked him here."

"Uh-huh," she murmured cynically. "You tracked him across the sand wastes."

"That's right," Danjer answered.

"Danjer could track a beetle in a sandstorm," Saxon spoke up proudly.

"Only if it was bright green," Danjer muttered under his breath.

"What's that?" The baroness' suspicious gaze shifted to Danjer.

"We thought he might have brought her here," Danjer voiced more clearly. "He knew you were looking for her. Can we see her?" he asked with a tight voice, trying to mask at least some of his concern.

For a few seconds, the baroness gave Danjer her bemused and curious attention. Then she leaned sideways and whispered to an attendant.

With her chin in her hand, the baroness watched the two captives as her attendant left with a guard. Her slow, lascivious gaze traveled the long hard limbs of their legs before it slid higher to take in their muscular forearms and broad shoulders.

Saxon rolled his big shoulders in a provocative display of male power as Danjer twisted his lips to hide his smile. For several moments the great hall was silent before the door opened again and the guard returned, shoving Jake into the room ahead of him.

Danjer's smile evaporated as his mouth flattened into a mean line.

Glowering backward at the man who'd propelled him into the hall, Jake took a step into the room—then froze when he saw the two men manacled at the post in the room's center. Carefully, he took a few more sideways steps, maintaining the distance that separated him from Danjer as he edged his way along the perimeter of the huge circular hall.

"Hello, Jake," Danjer said in a smooth, deadly voice. "We were just telling the baroness here, that we're musicians. I'm glad you could be here to back us up."

Jake nodded nervously, sliding a few more steps toward the baroness.

"Tell her we're musicians, Jake. Tell her the truth and I might let you live long enough to spend the gold she paid you for the imp—*if* Pink is unharmed."

Licking his lips nervously, Jake nodded again, and it was apparent to everyone in the large hall that Jake was terrified of the dark man who stood in the center of the room—regardless of the fact that he was shackled and chained to a huge post.

Unconsciously, the soldiers who guarded Danjer shuffled their feet as they put a few more inches between themselves and the intimidating captive. The baroness frowned at her soldiers. Cocking her head, she appeared to reconsider the handsome man who practically oozed a dark aura of cold, merciless violence before returning her gaze to the nervous young man who had brought her the imp.

"She's all right, Danjer. Pink's all right," he insisted anxiously.

"How did you get her here without harming her?" Danjer demanded, his voice like a knife. "She must have put up a fight."

Swiftly Jake shook is head, turning his hand, palm upward. "She s-slept all the way here. I injected her with this ring," he explained in a rush, demonstrating the ring's small needle on the inside of his hand. "I...j-just put my hand on her thigh," he said as Danjer glared at him. "It wasn't the gold," Jake pleaded in a hoarse voice. "I was just tired of being afraid, Danjer. I wanted out of the —"

But Danjer cut him off with a driven snarl of disgust. "Just tell the baroness we're musicians, Jake."

"I j-just wanted to get away, out of the country," Jake persisted.

"Then I hope she gave you a lot of gold, Jake. Enough gold for you to get far, far away...from me. Now tell her."

Jake continued to nod as he reached the relative safety of the baroness' side. "That's right," he croaked, his eyes darting to the baroness then back to Danjer. "They're musicians. Saxon and Danjer, of Hard and Fast."

"Musicians," the baroness imparted with a mocking smile, raking Danjer's long, muscled thighs with her loitering gaze. "Right," she drawled. "If you're musicians, I'm a virgin. If you're musicians...then I guess you ought to know a few love songs." With a snap of her fingers she signaled her attendant. "Get my quartet in here," she called out. A slow, malicious grin began to curl at the corner of her black-glossed mouth. "Bring the imp as well."

Doors opened and people rushed back and forth while the baroness smiled smugly and her musicians hurried in with their instruments. Danjer watched the door with keen vigilance and caught up a breath when Pink appeared in the opening.

She was still dressed in Chloe's long, creamy white gown. It fell from her shoulders and hugged the gentle curves of her body as it draped all the way to the ground. She appeared to be a little dazed. Maybe confused. But when her eyes found his, she started and choked out a small sound of surprise as her green eyes widened, first in relief as she realized he was alive, then with concern as she must have recognized he might not remain so for very much longer—considering the fact that he was now the baroness's prisoner.

Unthinkingly, he moved toward her, his chains clinking and holding as he swept her body with his hungry gaze. Finding her unharmed, his gaze settled questioningly on her face. When she turned her chin fractionally, he blew out a thankful sigh. They hadn't been able to make her orgasm—as yet.

The baroness's voice intruded into his evaluation as Pink's guards moved her to the foot of the dais. There, they pushed her to sit on the marble steps. "Why don't you sing your imp a love song?" the baroness suggested snidely. "I've a favorite tune. It's a bit melancholy but highly appropriate to the occasion, considering what I'm going to *do* to you *if* you can't sing."

Leaning forward with his arms stretched and bound behind him, Danjer glared from beneath the dark spill of his hair as the musicians milled about nervously. Chairs scraped as they were hastily dragged from the perimeter of the hall and the baroness's quartet got themselves arranged before the dais. Three men and one woman switched on their keytars and waited for the baroness to name her tune.

"A Love to Die For," the baroness announced to the silent assembly. Beside him, Danjer heard Saxon snuff out his snort of surprise. "It shouldn't give you any trouble if you are, as you claim to be, musicians."

"It won't give them any trouble," Pink spoke up quietly. She gave Danjer a proud smile as she fingered the thick copper necklace around her neck. The ring Saxon had given her was missing, no doubt stolen by the baroness's people.

In truth, Pink felt a little disoriented. The last thing she remembered was heading south on the back of Jake's bike. They'd traveled perhaps an hour before she must have fallen asleep. She'd no more than woken up in a depressingly familiar room when the baroness's people had turned up to escort her to the great hall.

She must have spent *hours* sleeping, she realized, as she looked out the windows into the sunlit yard.

As if in an attempt to shift everything back into place, she shook her head as her eyes clung to Danjer, drinking in the sight of his long, cleanly muscled limbs—uninjured, unbroken, unharmed. Saxon slouched safely beside him with an air of complete indifference, as though the fact that he was chained to a post didn't trouble him in the least. He didn't look like he was bluffing, either. When she caught his eye, he winked. She gave him an uncertain frown in return.

Turning her head, her gaze traveled behind her to the throne and the baroness, where Jake stood fidgeting at her side. She frowned as she followed his terrified gaze back to Danjer. Something was wrong. Surely...Jake hadn't betrayed his friends?

The idea had barely formed in her mind before she felt sorry for Jake.

Danjer would kill him.

Again she shook her head, surprised that she was more concerned for Jake's safety than either Saxon or Danjer's.

But then, Danjer was an Earther.

Passionate, violent, unpredictable. And — above all — inventive.

The music started with a short introduction before gently flowing into the melody. A few bars went unanswered before Danjer's voice picked up the following notes a little hesitantly. Leaning forward against the chains that bound him, his voice was quiet, his eyes downcast, fixed on the floor as he whispered the first words of the song. Then he tilted his head, shrugging and watching the ground as he picked up the second stanza a little more strongly. His eyebrows lifted as his eyes remained hugging the floor and he sang the song, almost apologetically, to the polished styrowood at his feet. Upon reaching the chorus, his voice strengthened and he flicked his gaze at Pink and then continued.

One by one, group by group, the occupants of the room stilled and quieted, conversation dropping off as their faces turned to the man chained in the center of the room. Again, his eyes flicked upward to catch at Pink's — then settled and locked on her gaze with sudden sureness. As his burning gaze fixed on her, the music rose and his voice rose with it, strong and male and full of deep, honest emotion. His rough-hewn voice caught at a tender word. Slowly, he blinked and resettled his eyes on Pink, continuing in quietly growing passion as he sang his song to the captive imp, closing his eyes during the rising chorus — apparently lost in the ballad — feeling his way through the high notes, now seemingly unaware of his audience and his venue.

Somewhere along the way the musicians had forgotten themselves as well and, moved by the raw energy of the singer, they threw themselves into the music, pulling in extra instrumentation in their effort to accompany the enigmatic vocalist. The music built and crashed into an awing crescendo as the keytarists tried to match the passion in Danjer's voice, the passion he brought to the song.

At the end of the third stanza, Saxon's eyes were lit with warm, admiring pride as he slid his back up the pole to take his place standing beside his friend. Danjer opened his eyes and flashed a smile at the man chained beside him, then pulled in a breath for the last verse. Together, they took up the final chorus as, chained together at the pole, their mouths moved together, separated by a scant few inches.

Saxon's glowing eyes rested on his friend for a few instants before swinging across the room to join Danjer's gaze and fasten on Pink—Saxon's voice taking the lower octave with a soft rich alto, harmonizing up until the final four words.

The music stopped and Danjer's eyes closed then opened to burn once more on Pink. Saxon smiled at his friend, pride firing his gaze while Danjer sang the last four words alone. "A love like yours."

Spellbound, Pink stared into Danjer's brilliant gaze, mesmerized by the expression haunting his handsome features. Somewhere in the large, silent hall somebody sniffled.

The baroness made a dismissive, impatient gesture in response. "Okay," she granted grudgingly, glaring at one of her keytarists who pressed a wrist beneath her nostrils. "You're musicians. At least, you certainly know how to put on a performance and sell a crowd. That's not the version I heard before the soundnet went out." She paused. "It's better." A heavy silence followed the baroness's words, full of expectation and churning emotion as Pink breathlessly waited to see what would happen next.

"Take the dark one to my rooms," the woman ordered abruptly. "Chain him within reach of my bed." Almost as an afterthought, she waved a manicured hand at Saxon. "Kill the other one," she added casually.

Pink's heart was suddenly in her throat, strangling the protest she tried to voice.

"No!" Danjer cut at the baroness as he was unshackled. "We live or die together," he said swiftly, backing into Saxon as he moved away from the guards who threatened him with their batons.

"Speak for yourself," Saxon muttered, cutting him an askance look and elbowing him forward.

Pink spoke up quickly as Saxon was unshackled and the two men stood shoulder to shoulder. "They work better in tandem," she told the baroness.

Danjer's jaw dropped and he stared at Pink while Saxon nodded vigorously, his gaze wide and hopeful as it swung to the baroness.

The baroness sighed as though bored. "Let's see what you're packing," she told them. Hesitantly, the two men exchanged glances. "Both of you," she clarified with an impatient wave of her hand.

Both Danjer and Saxon hooked their thumbs into the tops of their leathers and pulled the front of their pants downward, just far enough to expose the curling hair shading the thick roots of their penises.

The baroness's eyes widened a little, then dropped lower to check out the leather bunched beneath their thumbs, concealing the rest of the massed male equipment covered by their pants. She nodded suddenly. "Take them both to my rooms. Strip them down and chain them within reach of my bed. They can live for now. And for as long as they continue to amuse me."

The two bowmen kept their crossbows aimed at the captives while the two prod-wielding guards approached, their electrical batons crackling with a menacing white fire. As the guards moved to herd them away, Danjer shot the imp a narrow look of hope while Saxon smiled with a wink.

Then the men set their feet.

"We're not leaving this room without the imp," Danjer announced, turning his riveting gaze on the baroness. "But we'll help you get what you want before we leave," he rumbled, ignoring Pink's sudden gasp.

Chapter Thirteen

ᔕᓄ

The baroness cut Danjer a cold look of warning but waved a hand to stop the guards moving toward them. "How do you *know* what I want?"

Danjer inclined his chin, indicating the imp. "She told us. Told us what you did to her the last time you got your hands on her. We can help you get what you want," he repeated.

"Why would you want to do that?" the baroness asked with evil wariness.

"We'll do it in return for her release. We'll do it once. We'll make her orgasm. Then you let us go. All of us."

"Danjer, no!" Pink cried out while the baroness appeared to mull Danjer's proposal.

"She can't orgasm without us," Danjer rasped, pushing the baroness with the next lie that fell from his lips.

The elegant aristocrat arched a questioning eyebrow. "That's not scientifically possible."

"I'm not talking science. I'm talking emotions. You couldn't make her come before," he pointed out. "It has to be us. It has to be both of us."

"Why?"

"Because she's in love with us. An imp can only climax with two men she loves. We have to mount her at the same time."

"Is that true?" the baroness questioned the imp with a snide drawl.

Pink's cheeks flushed deep rose but she didn't answer.

"I don't want your fluids mixed with hers," the baroness argued after a moment's thought.

Danjer smiled, knowing the baroness's capitulation was at hand.

"We agree," Saxon spoke up. "We agree, don't we, Danjer? We'll use our fingers."

"Saxon," Pink pleaded as her eyes traveled anxiously between the two men. "Danjer, if you do this, thousands of men may lose their lives."

"I don't care about thousands of men!" Saxon countered.

Her chin came up, though it quivered with the barest tremble. "You care about Olan and Junkie."

Saxon hesitated. "Not that much," he said, gazing into her eyes and shaking his head. "Not as much as I care about you. Danjer?"

"Not that much," Danjer agreed quietly, pinning her with his gaze. "We're going to have to do this, Pink."

"But," she argued quickly, wetting her mouth with the tip of her tongue, "there's every chance she'll kill us anyway — afterward."

"Pink!" he cut at her. Masking the pride he felt for her, Danjer shot Pink a meaningful glare. "You're just going to have to trust me on this.

"I don't think she'll kill us," Danjer stated with quiet assurance. "At any rate, I'm willing to take my chances," he concluded, shifting his gaze to the aristocrat's watchfully narrowed eyes.

"Get ready," he advised the baroness, flashing her a wickedly male smile. "Because we'll be hard when we're done with the imp. After fucking her with our fingers, we'll be really hard. We'll need release. We can pump ourselves out...or we can save ourselves for you." Danjer gave the baroness a slow, sexy smile, filled with cool male arrogance and the promise of a hard, aggressive taking. "I hope you're ready for the ride of your life."

The baroness eyed the two men with interested speculation. "Is that part of the agreement?"

Danjer inclined his head. "We fuck the imp with our fingers. Then we fuck you." He let his gaze slide over the baroness's body in a tempting appraisal. "And afterward, we go free."

For several seconds, the baroness stared at him, her eyes drifting down to his crotch. As final encouragement, he reached down with one manacled hand to rearrange his package then dragged his flattened palm up over his fly.

"Chain the imp to the floor," the baroness ordered abruptly.

"What?" Saxon blurted as her personal guard moved immediately to carry out her order.

"You said you wouldn't leave the room without her," the baroness imparted with an evil, lazy smile. "I just want to make sure she stays in the room until she comes."

"Strip her first," the baroness told her men.

Metal links scraped and chinked as Danjer fought the men who held his chains. "*Let us,*" he protested as he struggled toward Pink.

"*You* don't move until the imp is chained," the baroness spat at him. "Bring my scientists," she told an attendant.

It took both guards as well as Saxon to hold Danjer back while the baroness's people stripped his woman. Moving Pink out into the center of the huge hall, the baroness's guards slashed her gown open and ripped her shorts from her before they forced her down to her knees. Snapping heavy iron manacles around her wrists, they looped a sharp, double-ended peg through the end of her chains. One of the baroness's personal guard took the axe at his belt and pinned her to the styrowood floor using the blunt end of his axe head to set the peg.

Naked but for her copper necklace, Pink knelt with her thighs spread wide, her arms stretched and fixed to the floor beside her folded legs, the short chains allowing her only a few inches of movement.

The light shafting through the hall's high windows limned Pink's sleek, feminine muscles. The sight of her staked out, trapped and helpless, her long, nude limbs spread in erotic display, was almost enough to drive Danjer mad. Fighting the men who held his chains, he threw himself at Pink. The sound of scraping metal ground through the hall as the iron bindings kept Danjer from reaching her.

Pink's eyes were panicked as she fought her chains, her shoulders jerking as her accusing glare slashed to his face. He froze beneath that green glare of frustration, shaking his head defensively as his lips formed her name.

As three white-clad scientists strode into the hall, Danjer and Saxon were finally released from their manacles. Their baton-wielding guards shoved them toward Pink. The two guards accompanied the captives, watching them closely, electrical prods at the ready as they stood behind them. In addition, each of them was still covered by a bowman who stood ten feet away, crossbow loaded with six iron bolts that promised abrupt death.

The fight went out of Pink's stiff shoulders and she slumped in defeat as Saxon fell to his knees beside her. "It's okay," he insisted with a whisper. "It's okay, Pink. Danjer and I have a plan," he said softly, cupping her chin in his big hand as he kissed her.

At his back, the baroness snorted at the big man's confident confession.

"Right now, we just need you to cooperate, sweetheart. The sooner you can come, the better. Don't fight it, love. Promise me you won't fight it." Moving his own legs apart, he fitted one of his knees inside hers as he held her face and kissed her mouth.

"That's right, Pink," Danjer reassured her, sliding down to his knees and wedging one of them between hers—alongside Saxon's—as they shielded her body from the baroness and her audience.

Then both men were kissing her, Danjer's lips pressing against one side of her mouth while Saxon rubbed his lips into the corner of the other side. Danjer's breath was rough, fiercely passionate as he fought for his share of her small mouth and Saxon murmured a deep groan of utterly male need.

She felt the warm presence of their testicles, wrapped in soft leather and resting against her folded knees as Danjer's fingers moved down across her belly and over the curls on her mound. Hesitating at the top of her cleft, he burrowed them gently between her fragile lips at the same time that Saxon's fingers tracked through her crease, skating over the crimp of her ass and continuing between her cheeks to find her tender opening. Involuntarily, she jumped at that initial rough contact of Saxon's hard fingers on the surface of her delicately lined entrance.

"Easy, sweetheart," he soothed. "You can do this, Pink. We love you."

"You can do this, Pink," Danjer whispered against her ear. "Open your eyes, sweetheart. Look at me, Pink. See how hard I am inside my leathers? How much I want you? Saxon and I are ready to spill, we want to get inside you so bad. It's almost killing us. But, Pink, I want you to orgasm on our fingers. Do you think you could do that?"

With her eyes on the huge bulge trapped inside Danjer's leathers, she nodded her head imperceptibly.

Danjer brushed his lips into her hairline, teasing her delicate feelers with the flirting press of his kiss. "Let us know when you're close," he whispered. This command was followed by a few more words of instruction whispered into her ear, then he mouthed her ear as he panted small words of promise between the darting wet forays of his tongue.

With his fingers stroking between her vulva and the kiss of her ass, Saxon groaned as his hips started to move, dragging the base of his leather-clad sex against Pink's trembling knees. At the same time, Danjer coaxed and loved the delicate bud of her clit with the rough tips of his fingers. His other hand was resting on her thigh as he let her feel his fingers tucked beneath his leathers and handling his own balls.

Again Saxon groaned, gasping as he cupped a hand under one of her plump breasts, lifting it to his mouth where he teased the hard knot of her nipple with the abrasive pad of his tongue.

A damp veil of sweat gleamed on her body as she trembled in the hands of her two lovers. She whimpered as they whispered promises of dark, hard, fulfilling completion, if she would only ask for it. If she would only give them the signal to take her cunt with the deep thrust of their fingers.

"Don't hold back," Saxon begged as his hand dropped from her breast and his palm drove down the hard, rigid line of his leather-strapped cock.

Her head fell back as her neck made a long arc and her body moved like a wave as she danced on the edge of release, strung out on pleasure, needing only their fingers to slide inside her before she'd start coming in dark, vicious waves of completion. When Danjer pulled his thumb over one of her feelers, she cried out in anguish.

"Get your people ready," Danjer shouted in a grunt. "Here she comes. Saxon!"

With those words, Saxon and Danjer each shoved two fingers deep inside her cunt.

Her head tossed wildly as the men stooped and dipped their faces, trying to follow her tossing head with theirs, fighting to land their mouths on hers, competing for the occasional mad touch of her lips. But before she'd finished climaxing, the guards were dragging them away from their woman as the baroness's people moved into the gap between her legs. Brandishing flat metal sticks, three scientists stooped to collect the imp's release as it seeped from her vagina and trickled over the swollen lips and folds of her sex.

Fighting their way back to her instinctively, the two men came up against the baroness's baton-wielding guards as the soldiers tried to keep them from their imp. Saxon landed a wild punch on a guard's mouth at the same time the cattle prod connected with his shoulder. He dropped to his knees, shouting in pain.

As Saxon hunched his shoulders in agony, the guard stumbled backward, shaking his head and licking his bloodied lip as he frowned at the people working between Pink's legs.

"No," Danjer screamed, fighting his way to Saxon. With one hand wrapped around the wrist of the other guard—twisting his baton away—Danjer shoved his fingers into the guard's mouth. "Now, Pink," he yelled.

"Attack the bowmen," Pink shouted, her face slashing left and right as she made eye contact with the two guards. Still licking at their lips where they found her intoxicating taste on their mouths, the two soldiers jumped to obey the imp.

As Saxon leapt to his feet, the guard nearest him threw himself at the bowman, ten feet distant, who held his crossbow cocked and aimed. Saxon raced in behind the guard, using the man as a shield. The bowman hesitated, trying to fix his sights on Saxon. At the last possible instant, the bowman turned his weapon ninety degrees, holding it away from his body as he loosed all six of his bolts in an attempt to hit Saxon. As Saxon dodged, three bolts thudded into the floor while the remaining three found deadly targets in the body of the baroness's guard.

Choking on his own blood, the guard slumped to his knees in front of Saxon as the blond warrior brought his huge fist around and floored the bowman. Ripping the bow from the soldier's hands, Saxon scrambled for the man's ammunition clip hanging from his belt. By the time Saxon had the crossbow reloaded, the second guard had disarmed the other bowman and was holding his crossbow. In the intervening time, Danjer had cleared a path between Saxon and the baroness, shoving her scientists to the floor. Saxon swung the weapon up to level on the baroness's chest.

Shouts originated in the corridor and more soldiers appeared at the open door but halted when they saw the crossbows targeting their mistress.

Finally, the baroness's personal guard reacted. Unfortunately for the baroness, the four men in her guard had apparently been chosen for their looks rather than either their brains *or* their brawn. Saxon loosed a single bolt and killed the first man who moved. "I've more than enough for the rest of you," he told the men who now hesitated, frozen in indecision as they stood on either side of their mistress.

The expression on the baroness's face was angry, stunned and impressed all at the same time. "You'll never get out of here alive," she stated firmly in the next breath. With one hand, she indicated the men blocking the hall's doorway. "There are fifty men between you and the palace doors."

"We're not going through the palace doors," Danjer laughed in answer, then pursed his lips to whistle. Seconds later there was a blast followed immediately by an explosion of light. Sharp sparks of flashing brightness filled the room as the huge hall windows imploded into a million raining shards of shattered glass.

The baroness stared as two bikes slid to a halt beside Danjer.

Swiftly, Danjer reached for a short pair of heavy wire cutters dangling from the belt swinging on his handlebars. With the wire cutters in one hand, he unclipped his handbow from his belt and hefted it in the other hand.

The baroness shook her head. "That was genius," she stated with awe. "Pure genius."

Danjer nodded proudly as his legs took him the few steps separating him from Pink. "It was Saxon's idea."

As Danjer cut the imp free and pulled her into his side, the baroness stared at Saxon, still standing in the center of the room. His legs were spread in a bracing stance and his crossbow was targeted on her chest.

"Why," Saxon rumbled, "does everybody think I'm an...an..."

"Imbecile?" Danjer offered.

"No..."

"Idiot?" Pink gave him the word with a fond smile.

"Yeah," Saxon drawled. "Why does everybody think I'm an idiot? My sense of direction might be a bit whacked and I may lose a few words sometimes, but I'm not stupid."

"I'll take those," Danjer insisted in the next breath, striding forward and collecting the flat metal instruments from the baroness' scientists, taking a moment to spit on them before he shoved them into the top of his leggings. "I'll take your lab jacket as well," he informed one of the scientists who quickly divested herself of the long white coat. This Danjer wrapped around Pink.

With the samples secured and Pink covered inside the crisp white jacket, Danjer turned to face the baroness. "You're coming with us," he informed her.

Glaring back at him, the baroness pressed her lips together.

"You can either come with us alive or stay here dead," Danjer informed her in no uncertain terms.

The baroness's eyes nicked across the room to where Saxon stood, his crossbow still targeting her chest. "You wouldn't kill an unarmed woman," she stated tentatively.

"Jake!" Danjer barked as he lifted his small handbow and leveled it at the baroness.

The younger man flinched. "He'll d-do it," Jake stammered as he rushed to tell her. "Earthers are...are animals when they're provoked. He'll kill you in a heartbeat."

Danjer grinned mirthlessly. "And then your heart will never beat again."

"He k-killed the Silver Duke...and his men," Jake told her.

Saxon lifted the nose of his crossbow. "I helped," he pointed out, cutting an askance glance at Jake.

"He killed the duke with his bare hands," Jake went on. "He *destroyed* a giant tick with nothing but a knife."

Saxon's jaw dropped at Jake's exaggeration—as well as his omission. Slowly, he shook his head as his handsome face wrinkled up in disgust.

Still the baroness hesitated. "The men on the walls won't open the gates."

"They will if they think we're going to kill you."

"The men in the gatehouse are 'droids," she argued nervously, now clearly concerned that she might die if the 'droids refused to open the gates. "They only respond to voice commands from their superiors. Threatening to kill me won't get the gates open."

"Then you'll give them a voice command," Danjer countered.

"They'll never hear me from inside the gatehouse tower."

Danjer and Saxon exchanged a brief, nasty smile. "Good thing we brought our own sound system," Saxon said with a grin.

Returning his wire cutters to his belt, Danjer punched open a saddlecase and reached inside for the head of the keytar—the long piece capped by the microphone. "You can tell your 'droids to leave the gates open," Danjer mentioned casually. "And they might as well lay down their arms at the same time. I'm expecting some friends soon. Have you met the Iron Duke?"

Horrified, the baroness shook her head.

"Well, you're about to."

Frustration and rage ate at the baroness's face, turning her lovely features into an ugly mask of fury. Her angry eyes cut to Jake then back to Danjer.

Danjer nodded. "If you haven't figured it out yet, we're musicians *and* soldiers," he told her.

Chapter Fourteen

ଽ**ଠ**

Danjer stood beside Pink in the great hall of his newly acquired villa, a gift from the queen in appreciation for his services in the war. The hall was long and well lit with large windows through which the afternoon sun fell to splash on the tiled floor. The walls were textured stucco and painted a soft white. But the floors beneath his feet were tiled with pink marble.

He liked the large windows. And the thick walls. But most of all he liked the old marble floors. As he gazed through the south-facing windows, the mountains rose on his right. A dense green forest stood behind the house and snaked down the east side of his property. Straight ahead were open fields of long grass which led to the distant sand wastes.

A month had passed since the baroness had ordered the palace gates open. No doubt, the edge of his sword tucked under her chin had been a great inducement. And the microphone on Saxon's keytar had definitely come in handy. The gates had swung inward at her command and that was how Au'Banner had found them when he'd arrived with his army an hour later.

The baroness had been removed from her station and would henceforth be spending the rest of her days incarcerated in a comfortable tower at Iverannon, which the queen was happy to provide for her. The queen had offered Danjer the baroness's palace, along with the title of Copper Duke, but Danjer had quickly refused. He didn't want be tied to a large property that he couldn't walk away from whenever the whim took him. Instead he'd settled for a sprawling villa tucked up against the mountains, south of Aranthea. He was planning the addition of a recording studio.

He already had a staff—of one. Pink's new guard. The guard who had been bound to Pink after tasting her release—the one who hadn't been killed by the baroness's bowman—had followed her to the villa. Briefly, Pink had considered ordering Molera to return happily to his past life. But the career soldier didn't appear to have a past life of any note, nor any family to speak of. He joined Danjer's staff.

Danjer was pleased to learn the man had some experience making brandy.

Smiling down at the woman beside him, Danjer realized he should probably check out the rest of his new property but he was too content—immensely content within this moment. Standing at her side. In his home. Alone with her.

Saxon was off exploring the grounds with Molera. It was a large property. With any luck, he'd be gone a long time.

The bedrooms would be upstairs, he told himself as he reached for her hand and lifted it to his lips, dragging his mouth slowly over her fingers, reveling in the pleasure of her smooth skin against his lips, drinking in the silken texture of her slender fingers.

Saxon had been right about her. There wasn't a place on her that wasn't soft.

With his other hand, he pulled her against his body and tilted his head as he nudged his lips against hers and slid his tongue into the small, pink kiss of her dainty mouth.

As he probed the moist, inner recesses—his cock warmed to aching by her shivering moan—he planned her slow seduction. He'd carry her up the stairs and lay her out on the bed. Sitting down beside her, he'd tug the bottom of her blouse from the top of her leggings. Taking his time, he'd unbutton her shirt from the bottom up and lay it open to showcase her pert, pink-nippled breasts before he went to work unfastening her pants.

"You're hard," she murmured around the brush and sweep of his tongue.

He nodded. "I want you," he whispered. "I want you," he repeated. "I want you beneath me, my cock stretching your pussy as I ride you. I want you to spread your legs for *me*. To wrap your legs around *my* hips. I want to take you as a man takes his woman. The woman he loves."

The sound of approaching cleats on styrowood interrupted this breathless confession.

So much for luck.

Pushing out a sigh, Danjer turned to watch the archway while Pink palmed his flanks provocatively.

"Not bad for a starter home," Saxon announced appreciatively, stepping through the arch as he gazed back over his shoulder into the entry. Glancing around the long room, he crossed the sun-washed floor to join his friends. "So how does it feel to be a Lord?"

"It's nice to finally be your *equal*," Danjer answered as he held Pink's hips, sealing her belly against the iron-hard length of his erection.

Saxon rubbed a hand over the front of his leathers. "You'll need another inch if that's what you're going for!" Saxon laughed as Danjer rolled his eyes with a stingy smile curving the rugged line of his lips.

Pulling away from Danjer, a small ridge formed between Pink's expressive eyebrows. "You're a Lord? Lord Saxon?" she questioned with quiet awe.

"Yeah," Saxon laughed with a crooked grin. "But I was born that way, so it hardly counts."

"Saxon's family has properties up and down the coast," Danjer informed her, grimacing uncomfortably as he palmed his erection to one side.

"The...coast?" she queried weakly. "But...I love the sea."

"We'll have to make a trip then." Saxon smiled, his gaze warm as he stared at her. "I want you to meet my family, anyhow." He hesitated, making sure he had Danjer's attention.

"We might as well get married while we're out there," he stated carefully.

When Danjer turned away without commenting, Saxon continued. "My parents will be pleased. They'll be getting a new daughter...as well as another son. My mother especially likes Danjer and she'll love you, Pink."

But Danjer didn't get a chance to remark on that comment because a slender man stood in the archway through which Saxon had just entered. Danjer cut a glance at him before crossing the room to the long aluminum bar against the east wall. The entire vertical surface of the hammered metal bar was embossed with a detailed battle scene commemorating some ancient victory. Reaching for a bottle, Danjer poured a drink. "What are you doing here?" he asked quietly.

"I'm tired of being afraid," Jake started. "I'm not a soldier, Danjer. I'm not like you and Saxon. I was afraid during every second of every battle we ever fought. Now the war's finally over and...I'm still afraid. I'll spend the rest of my life afraid, wondering when you're going to come after me and kill me." He took a deep breath. "If you're going to kill me, do it now, Danjer. Because I'd rather be dead than live out the rest of my life in fear."

Danjer shook his head slowly as he turned from the bar, the short glass in his hand. "I'm not going to kill you, Jake. I might have, if Pink had come to any harm. Some men should never go to war. You're one of them. You're a musician, not a soldier. But I'll tell you something about yourself, Jake. Something you don't know." Sauntering across the room, he put the glass in Jake's hand.

"Even as scared as you were in the baroness's hall, you'd never have let Pink come to any harm. And if the baroness had ordered my death, you'd have stepped between her bowman and me. You'd have done the same for Saxon."

Jake hung his head. "I...I'd like to think so, Danjer."

"Thank you for the truth, Jake, when you told the baroness we were musicians. And thank you for the lie, when you told the baroness we'd kill her, unarmed though she was." Danjer put his hand on the young man's shoulder. "I want you to join my staff, here at the villa. I want you in the band. I want you to join Hard and Fast."

Jake lowered his head, shaking it. "Fuck," he scratched out hoarsely. "Fuck, you're a bastard, Danjer." He lifted his face and there were tears on it. "What will the guys think—about what happened at the Copper Palace—about what I did?"

"Oh hell," Danjer snorted. "They think we planned the whole thing—the four of us—to get into the palace and take out the baroness."

For several seconds Jake looked like he would crumple. Very determinedly, Danjer continued to smile at him.

"Thank you," Jake finally said. Lifting his drink, he threw the liquor down his throat then put the glass back in Danjer's hand, grasping it for several seconds before he turned and strode from the room.

Danjer blew out a sigh and looked at Saxon, smiling quietly beside him. "He's just a kid," Danjer told him.

Saxon nodded in the direction of the open archway. "I reckon he'll die now, before he lets anything happen to you or yours. I think you may have just made Jake a brave man."

Danjer was quiet as he considered the empty arch. Seconds ticked by as the silence thickened. His cock pulsed meaningfully as the room grew heavy with still, weighty expectancy. He took in a long, slow breath of air. It tasted like sex.

Finally Saxon broke the tense silence. "Tried out the bedroom yet?"

He shook his head.

"Waiting for me?" the blond rumbled in a voice cut with sensual undertones.

"You wish," Danjer imparted with a surly growl.

"Don't you think we should?"

Danjer strained to smile as Saxon moved between Pink and him, putting his long golden body against hers and crowding into her as he nudged her slowly away from Danjer toward the open arch. Watching with clenched teeth, Danjer felt his blood thicken and his breathing quicken as his cock thrummed and stretched within the black leathers that wrapped his hips. When the two of them disappeared through the arch, he followed. And caught up to them between the arch and the foot of the staircase.

Reaching for Pink's arm, Danjer turned her away from Saxon.

He knew it was wrong, but he resented Saxon. Resented his presence in his home. The first home he'd ever had. He knew he shouldn't feel that way. He knew he didn't have the right to feel that way. Saxon had always shared everything he owned with Danjer — without even thinking about it. Without even realizing he was giving anything up.

Including Pink.

But Danjer resented him, nonetheless. This was *his* home. And he wanted to take *his* woman in *his* home, in *his* bedroom.

Alone with the woman he loved.

Jeezis Skies, he wanted her. And for *just* this *once*, he didn't want Saxon around. For just once, he wanted to pretend that Saxon didn't exist. That it was just him and Pink. That it was just him claiming her with his cock.

Pulling Pink into his body, Danjer tipped her head back and covered her mouth with a branding kiss. Seconds later, he was lost to her taste and texture, mauling her mouth hungrily as he pressed his tongue through her lips to claim the moist envelope with utter male dominance — leaving no opening for his best friend standing a foot distant.

His hands moved restlessly down her back, possessively, claiming her as his own, marking her with his rough grasp, grabbing at her ass and squeezing the curving globes in his hands as he pulled her tight against his lower body and ground his thick erection into her firm belly. Giving himself over to passionate aggression, he groaned helplessly as he continued the kiss, demanding her lips, dominating her mouth as his desperate hands searched blindly for a path into her clothing. Fumbling with the thin cotton top she wore tucked into her leggings, he moaned like a helpless addict, drugged with lust, his thinking nowhere near clear enough to fathom complicated things like buttons and clasps.

As he twisted his mouth over hers, rubbing his wet lips into her open-mouthed kiss, his eager hands brushed up against large male fingers. Unwilling to acknowledge Saxon's presence, he ignored Saxon's trespassing touch as he repositioned his lips over hers and swallowed her sobbing breath into his lungs.

The next time he opened his eyes, her pert-nippled breasts were naked and he stared down at them in wonder. Both stunned and pleased to find them exposed and ready for his grasp, he brought his hands around to cup them and love them as he lowered his head to suck a puffy nipple gently between his teeth. She cried out and arched into his hold as he captured her nipple with his tongue and played the stiff bud against the roof of his mouth. When she whimpered, he opened his eyes to take in her face and then lowered his gaze again to the mounded perfection of her breasts and the flowering pink blush his stubbled jaw had flushed out on her shell-pale flesh.

At the periphery of his vision, he was vaguely aware of large hands sliding down her legs — hands that were sprinkled with fine, gold hair — pushing her pants to her calves and lifting her delicate ankles free of her leggings.

Her clothes were coming off.

Through the carnal haze that fogged his mind, he was barely aware of how this was happening. All he knew was that her clothes were being removed. That was all that mattered.

Then she was finally nude. Beautifully smooth and silky wherever he touched her as his hands glided everywhere they could reach and he absorbed her satin warmth on the open palms of his hands. His cock throbbed, an aching mass strangling inside his leathers as he was obsessed with a singular need. He wanted to plant her. He wanted to stretch her on his body and stake her on his dick, his pulsing flesh buried to the root, deep inside her hot, quivering cunt. He wanted her with an animal urgency he couldn't deny or control.

Then and there. Here and now.

In the middle of the entry.

Slowly, she was drifting away from him and, without realizing it, he was going with her, following her, keeping his body against hers, his lips on her mouth and his tongue probing restlessly between her teeth, using it to fuck her mouth in the same way he wanted to take her cunt.

As though leashed to a breeding female, he followed her like a male animal on a chain—helplessly panting and almost frothing with need, mad for his chance to mate her.

Like an untried youth in thrall to the scent of a virgin cunt, Danjer followed his woman across the tiled entry, grasping her hips and praying for the instant she would taunt him with the press of her pussy as she begged to be mounted. Begged wordlessly as she pushed her sex at him. Begged to be fucked hard. Giving him the signal to climb onto her and drive his cock up through her tender slot all the way to the back of her cunt.

Gulping for each breath that racked his lungs, Danjer followed her as Saxon moved her away from him.

Abruptly, his shins came up against the stairs and he took a gasping breath as he fell to his knees onto the second step. Startled, he found himself with his face in her chest, gazing at the delicate color of her pink-tipped breasts. When he let his gaze drop, he found her thighs stretched over Saxon's as he sat on the stairs. Vaguely, he wondered when Saxon had removed his leathers.

The golden warrior held her captured on his lap, facing outward, her legs spread over the thick muscles of his open thighs. Her pussy was stretched indecently wide, her labia deep and rosy, parted in an erotic invitation.

Stifling a needy moan, Danjer moved between Saxon's spread legs, reaching for her damp flesh with his hand, trailing a finger slowly through the folded wet fire stretched inside her precious cunt, collecting her slick, molten honey as he dipped a single finger into her hourglass opening and watched her buck, staked out on the spread of Saxon's huge frame.

Helpless and exposed, trapped in ecstasy, she writhed before him. When he removed his finger from her fluttering cunt, he pushed his fingers higher, through her folds to her clitoris where he pinched the nub gently. Hot and wet, she gushed around his fingers, her cunt welcoming his touch as her musky scent, tempting and intoxicating, filled the humid air between their sweat-damp bodies.

He drew in a slow, ragged breath and filled his lungs with her unique scent, flavored with her sweet sex, smelling and tasting like the promise of heaven—rich and fragrant and darkly addictive, like some thick, heady liqueur.

Lost in a sex-hazed trance of need, he wanted more. He wanted her taste on his tongue. He wanted to bury his face in her cunt and lick her to completion. Sliding down a step, he moved his face between her legs and opened his mouth.

Distantly, he was aware of Saxon asking, "Do you want protection, Pink?" He felt her shake her head just before Saxon shouted, "Danjer!"

As the deep male voice intruded into his lust-induced stupor, Danjer hesitated. He licked his lips longingly as he watched her glistening vulva, inches from his mouth. His sex-clouded brain moved his lips closer to the deep pink of her sex, the beckoning scent of her delectable pussy.

"Danjer," Saxon repeated, "no."

Danjer shook his head, full and heavy and foggy with lusty cobwebs. "Fuck you," he murmured as he gazed at the enticing sight of her long, streaming entrance. Her scent filled his senses and, like a moth, he was drawn to her burning, wet flame.

And there was more—more than just the raw, burning ache of hunger. From behind the haze of need clouding his mind and blurring his vision, Danjer saw this step as a way out. A path to happiness through oblivion. One taste of the imp's come and he'd be free. Finally free of the grudging resentment and envious greed that had been dogging him ever since he'd set eyes on her. One kiss and he would achieve acceptance—his own acceptance of the man he would forever have to share his love with. With his mouth open, he touched his lips to her cleft.

Then Saxon's fist was beneath his chin. "I won't let you do this," Saxon told him. "Get your dick out," he urged gently. "Give her your cock."

With his eyes glued to Pink's pussy, Danjer tried to shake himself free as he moved his mouth again to the rosy folds tucked between the lips of her sex.

"Tell him, Pink," Saxon ordered in a voice that was suddenly insistent. "Tell him that you want to be mounted and fucked."

"Yes," Pink sobbed, uneven desperation in her voice.

Danjer's eyes jerked to her face as she strained in Saxon's hold.

"Mount me, Danjer. I don't want your kisses. I want your cock."

Blinking uncertainly, he shook his head as Pink squirmed evocatively within the tight constraint of Saxon's hold.

"Give me your cock," she begged. "I want your shaft buried inside me."

Abruptly, the decision to kiss or fuck was taken out of Danjer's hands as Saxon lifted and turned her. A sudden fire of anger surged inside him as Saxon took control of the situation — took the control away *from him*. Saxon's knees were now between Pink's legs, pushing them open as she stood on the floor at the bottom of the stairs. Danjer growled as he watched Saxon kissing her mouth before he pressed her face lower, into his groin.

Saxon's gaze was uncompromising as he lifted his eyes to Danjer. "Mount her," he commanded.

What the fuck. Damn Saxon for his interference.

Danjer's eyes narrowed on his friend. "Okay," he said finally, coldly. Wrapping his big hands around Pink's hips, Danjer yanked her backside toward him. Shoving his feet between hers, he urged her legs farther apart. With his eyes glued to her crease as it opened, he watched her glistening vulva widen as he clutched both globes of her ass, pulling her cheeks apart and stretching her hourglass wider as moisture gathered at the base of the rosy slit and seeped, shining, into the seam of her sex.

Wrenching his fly open and pushing his jockstrap down, he lifted out the dark weight of his erection, then pulled his hips back to bring his cock head to the shuddering, wet mouth of her pussy. He fitted the broad, dark head against her entrance, swabbing the soft, wet velvet of her vulva with the harsh angry head of his cock. "Okay," he muttered in a deep growl. "You asked for it." He let her cheeks ease closed around his smooth crown as he reached down and palmed the back of her thighs, then dragged his hands up over the cheeks of her ass. Again he met Saxon's gaze. "But I want her to watch this."

Pink gasped as Danjer pressed the hot width of his cock head against her opening. With a sob of relief, she curled her tongue around the tip of Saxon's cock, inexpressibly thankful for the big man's intervention. Saxon had distracted Danjer and stopped him from taking the kiss that would bind him to her as completely as the unfortunate zombie guard who'd followed her from the Copper Palace. Rooting the tip of her tongue into the slit on his cock head, she sucked on Saxon's first wide inches. But Saxon lifted her mouth from his cock. As he pulled her chin up, she reached for his cock with her tongue, lapping at the salty moisture on his blunt tip.

"Don't you want to see this?" he asked her gently. "Don't you want to watch Danjer as he mounts you?"

Catching her bottom lip in her teeth, she stared into Saxon's loving gaze an instant before she turned her head to look over her shoulder. She could have kissed both men for this permission to follow her own wanton impulse. Her hair fell over one eye and she felt Saxon's fingers pulling her long fringe out of her eyes.

Danjer caught her warm stare within the fierce light of his own gaze. He shook his head and his damp hair shifted on his shoulders before he lowered his eyes to his groin and fed the huge width of his cock into her slim vulva.

She felt the delicate skin of her opening pull and stretch as he pushed into her and heard his murmured growl of masculine approval as his thick root scraped at the sensitive flesh that rimmed her hungry slit. Then he shafted her in one long, even thrust. When he banged up against her cervix, she lost control. As he stood behind her with his cock head fully seated at the back of her cunt, she caught a glimpse of his face just before she lost herself to carnal mania. Danjer's expression was one of dark, evocative hunger as he watched her body contort on his cock. As his fingers gouged into her flanks, holding her into the fuck, she buried her face again in Saxon's lap. Screaming hoarsely, she entered an open-ended orgasm.

His eyes were on fire as he shafted her with the forging lunge of his hips and she danced on the end of his dick, orgasming without closure. He wrenched his cock back several inches then slammed into her again. "You asked for it," he grated, pushing out a short, rough breath. "Saxon," he growled, "her clit."

Pink felt Saxon's hand smooth down over her mound and slip inside her labia. With Saxon's fingers manipulating her clitoris and Danjer crammed in to his balls, his fat cock head lodged against the back of her cunt, Pink screamed and jumped in the clasp of his biting grasp. Instinctively, she rocked back to meet his thrusts as he delivered each punishing stroke—hard and deep, short and jabbing—as his thumbs sank bruisingly deep into the soft cushion of her ass, pulling her open and stretching her rim with rough, abrasive pleasure.

She cried helplessly as he held her there, trapped forever on the edge of shattering pleasure, as he pounded into her with a starkly brutal animal intensity. At the same time, Saxon cradled her head in his lap, his hips undulating gently as he rubbed his massive cock against her damp face, and his fingers danced lightly over her clitoris.

"Danjer."

Pink heard Saxon finally intervene over the raw sound of her own helpless cries.

"Let her come."

"*Don't* interfere," Danjer gritted as he slammed against her. "She asked for it. You *both* asked for it."

Saxon growled warningly. "Give her your finger, Danjer. *Now*! Or I'll give her mine."

"You will *not* come between us Saxon! Not this time."

"Stop it, Danjer! You're *torturing* her."

"She asked for it," Danjer bit out, as he continued driving against her, almost overcome with resentment, watching Pink straining in his hands, her body racked by erotic convulsions—punishing her. Punishing her for Saxon's presence and interference.

"She was just trying to stop you from kissing her!" Saxon shouted. "From binding yourself to her!"

"No!" Danjer screamed, planting his cock at the back of her vagina and holding her shimmering body on his dick, his hands slipping on her hips, slick with her warm, scented sweat.

Saxon's next words were terrifyingly calm.

"Does this make you feel powerful, Danjer? Is that why you're doing this?" Saxon didn't sneer, although he might have. There was no cruelty in his voice. There was only quiet strength.

Damn Saxon for his goodness. Fuck Saxon to hell and back.

"No!" he shouted, hating Saxon for his kindness, his gentleness, his generosity. Not wanting to meet his eyes.

Ashamed of himself and his actions.

"Danjer," Saxon cut in calmly, "look at me."

Squeezing his eyes shut, Danjer opened them again to meet Saxon's commanding gaze.

"Don't do this to her."

An angry shout tore past his lips as Danjer thrust himself from Pink, his cock swinging heavy and wet, as he glared at Saxon. Panting with frustration, he reached up with one sweaty wrist to move his dark hair off his face. "Okay, Saxon," Danjer threw at him. "Have it your way," he snarled. With those words, he wrapped his fingers around his shaft as he pumped his cock, riding his fist up its length until his shining semen bled from his slit in a thin wash. "You want to fuck her without me?" he shouted. "Go ahead!" he roared.

Saxon gave him a stern look of reproach as he shook his head and turned Pink on his lap again. Her pale, slender body was wrung out and limp as Saxon stretched her on his body a second time. Her head rolled back on Saxon's shoulder as she sucked in tiny, rapid breaths, her face turned, her lips moving against the thick, corded column of Saxon's throat.

The room seemed to darken as Danjer stood at the bottom of the stairs, his legs spread wide, his cock in his hand, his body crushed with dark need, his emotions still edged with anger and resentment as he watched Pink's small kiss of a mouth move against Saxon's neck—his heart breaking with remorse as his gaze moved lower, over her limp, ravaged body.

Carefully, Saxon eased her legs over his again. "That's not what this is about, Danjer. And you know it.

"Come," Saxon told him. "We'll do this together. Fuck her like you love her. Gently," he reminded him.

With the wary instincts of an animal rebuked, Danjer held back, his gaze narrowed on Pink's damp face as her head turned on Saxon's shoulder. Her quiet gaze lifted to his and he was almost undone by the understanding and acceptance he found in the generous green glow of her eyes—the simple unconditional love that glimmered in the quiet depths of her forgiving gaze.

"Pink," he rasped in a raw, pleading voice. He hoped it sounded like an apology, because it sure as hell felt like one. That single difficult word felt like it had been ripped from his soul and torn from his heart.

"Danjer," she answered with a wan smile. "Come."

Although Danjer had fought to refuse Saxon's command, he couldn't refuse the woman. He couldn't refuse Pink. He couldn't turn down the shining pink slit of her cunt and the wet heat of her pussy, the promise of release in the tight clamp of her climaxing channel. He needed her velvet fire surrounding his sex. Approaching her open legs, he guided his streaming cock head through the swollen lips of her pussy, toward her slippery entrance. He probed for her notch blindly as Saxon lifted her several inches then eased her down onto his own shaft.

She went suddenly mad as Saxon penetrated her—and Danjer lost her. Choking with need, he slid his hand between her legs, groping desperately, searching for her opening as his fingers skidded through her wet folds to scrape against Saxon's rough, damp testicles.

"Fuck," he bit out in frustration as he tried to get on her. Then Saxon's hand was at the base of his sex, cupping his balls as Saxon reached under his own leg and drew him to her opening. Saxon's fingers coaxed him firmly between Pink's open legs and fed Danjer's dick into her cunt.

Strangling a raw cry of relief and pleasure, Danjer sank inside her. Saxon's earlier appeal for caution and reserve was lost to lust as Danjer started driving against her, pulling his hips and slamming into her as she sat impaled on Saxon's thick cock. The giant blond held her shafted on his massive steel, held her writhing body in place to receive Danjer's savage thrusts, her cunt stretched wide and positioned where Danjer could ream into her as he flexed his knees and drove against her.

Again and again, Danjer crushed into her hot channel, his hands clutching Saxon's sweat-dampened thighs just above the knees, the rounded crown of his glans riding up and down the length of Saxon's shaft until Saxon was roaring and coming and Pink was screaming and coming—all at the same time. Everything was incredibly hot and wet as Danjer's cock was bathed in Pink's sweet female honey and Saxon's wash of male release. Jerking his hips, he rammed into her a last time and held hard and fast inside her, choking as he leaned forward, his lips joining Saxon's as he buried his mouth against Pink's neck.

Saxon's lips moved against his as Danjer came in hard, driving surges. He trembled as he sucked at Pink's delicate flesh, almost overcome with excess emotion. Saxon's hand was on the back of his head as his open mouth moved in a damp line across Danjer's jaw.

Feeling drained to the point of exhaustion, Danjer pulled in a deep breath and lifted his face out of Pink's neck. He met Saxon's green gaze as Saxon questioned him with his solemn expression. "Are you all right?" he asked him.

Danjer didn't answer — because Danjer didn't know. He had never felt more fucking confused in his life. He hated himself for what he'd done to Pink. For what he'd almost done. Orgasm was intensely pleasurable. But how long could a woman climax without going mad? How long could she continue like that, flogging herself to death, impaled on a man's dick?

He hated Saxon for being the strong one.

At the same time, he loved Saxon more than ever.

Great, good, gentle Saxon had taken control when control had been required. When Danjer had been lost in his lust and his anger and his violent driving need to leave his mark on the girl, Saxon had stood true — cool and firm — helping him to find the love buried deep in his lust, reminding him of the devotion that fired his violent passion.

Saxon had stopped him when he might have harmed her. For that he would be forever grateful. And Saxon had stopped Danjer before he could harm *himself*. When Danjer had been ready to sacrifice his free will, Saxon had stood strong and commanding. Saxon had prevented him from taking that irrevocable step while in a fevered state of lust-driven anticipation, blinded by his carnal need.

Danjer groaned as he rubbed his burning eyes into Pink's temple.

The worst of it was the realization that *he couldn't do this without Saxon*. He couldn't love Pink without his best friend's strength to protect them. Unfortunately, he didn't think he could love her *with* his best friend.

Which brought him back to irrevocable steps...and the imp's kiss.

The more Danjer thought about it, the more it seemed like the only way out.

Chapter Fifteen

ဢ

They spent the rest of the afternoon together, walking Danjer's new property lines. Saxon held Pink's hand as Danjer trailed them moodily. Pink gave him his space and his time, hoping for a private moment later in the day. They didn't get that moment until the day's end. Early evening found Pink with Danjer in the bedroom he had chosen for himself. They'd left Saxon in the kitchen. He'd promised dinner in an hour.

"Can Saxon cook?" Pink asked Danjer.

Danjer perched his butt on the long, low cabinets built beneath the wide, tinted windows spanning the south wall of his bedroom. Behind him the skies were dark as a storm gathered in the east, ready to make its westward run.

Although she stood only feet from where he leaned against the cabinet, Pink felt as though a great, terrible distance separated them. Something had changed and it frightened her. Something had changed when she'd acted to stop him from taking that life-altering kiss, when she'd pushed him to mount her on the stairs. She was afraid of the emotions that she'd unleashed in him — not the vicious side of his nature — it wasn't that. Instead, she feared the dark, moody, unforgiving side of his personality. She feared that he'd done something for which he might not be able to forgive himself. Something that he might not be able to forget or put behind him. At the same time, she wondered how often this situation would replay itself in the future as Danjer struggled to overcome his dark emotions and fight his instinct for domination.

He'd been quiet and distant all afternoon. She was scared. Afraid of the tension that surrounded him like a black shroud, afraid of the strain her presence was putting on his relationship with Saxon. Afraid of losing him. Afraid of losing them both.

Reaching for him, she touched his arm.

He jolted at her touch, as though he'd forgotten she was there.

"Can Saxon cook?" she asked again.

Pulling her between his spread legs, his hand slid inside her cotton blouse as he fingered her belly ring with his thumb. For several seconds he watched his thumb move over the sparkling stone. "He's memorized a few recipes," he told her distractedly. "He's okay as long as there aren't any ingredients like...tarragon or manalasta."

"And if there are?"

"He'll come up here and ask for help remembering."

Danjer lapsed into silence again as he continued to stroke his thumb over the dimple of her belly. His eyes were downcast and his expression edged with discontent. Finally he spoke. "Saxon is...gentle," he stated.

She nodded in answer.

"He's gentle with you."

Again she nodded.

"I should be gentler," he stated as his unhappy gaze met hers.

She shook her head quickly. "I like the way Saxon makes love to me," she told him softly. "But I love the way you...take me. I love your passion and even your violence. I love your arms around me, crushing me. I love your cock inside me beating against my dark spot, wrenching me into submission...and orgasm." She gave him a soft smile, sifting her fingers through the dark silk of his thick hair. "Please don't apologize for what happened this afternoon. I loved what you did to me. I loved every long, anguished second of it."

Danjer shook his head. "It's not only that," he told her. "I wish I could *love* you the way Saxon loves you. I wish I could share you — happily — the way he does. I don't understand how he can do it. How he can share you with me without wanting to...to kill me," he pushed out with a wry laugh.

"Don't you?" she asked him, tilting her head as she tried to capture his gaze. "Don't you understand, Danjer? Saxon *loves* you."

Some unnamed emotion trembled across the hard line of his beautiful mouth before firming into a grim line. "No more than I love him. But that doesn't stop me from wanting to destroy him when he touches you."

Pink shook her head. "You don't understand. Saxon isn't sharing *me* any more than he's sharing you. He loves you as much as he does me. When he makes love to me, he's making love to you as well. Saxon would never consider taking me alone. He wouldn't betray your love for him...or what he feels for you."

Danjer stared at her uncertainly. "No," he said. "Saxon is as...masculine as I am. Saxon doesn't *love* me. Not the way you're saying. Not like that."

"I understand what you're trying to tell me, Danjer. But I'm not certain that there's more than one kind of love."

Moving her hair out of her eyes and tucking it behind one ear, Danjer searched her gaze. As his calloused thumb scraped at the shell of her ear, she thought she heard the door unlatch. She tilted her head to listen but a distant rumble of thunder filled the room at almost the same moment.

"It doesn't make any difference," Danjer said finally. "None of it makes any difference because none of it makes it any easier to share you," he said, a sad smile edging the hard lines of his mouth. "It grows harder all the time." He shook his head. "I don't want to lose Saxon. But...I don't think I can share you anymore," he laughed quietly without humor. "*Anymore*? I didn't want to share you in the first place."

Her heart almost stopped. "Are you asking me to choose, Danjer? To choose between you and Saxon?"

The question seemed to take him by surprise. "No," he murmured quickly. "No. I'm asking you to let me bind myself to you."

"Danjer!"

"No. Listen. Hear me out before you turn me down." He stopped a moment, his starkly handsome face troubled as he gathered his argument. "I love you, Pink. And I'd do anything for you anyhow, without the imp's kiss. I'd do anything for your happiness, so I don't see what difference it would make if I tasted you. I don't know how anyone would be able to tell the difference. The only difference would be that...I might be happy. Or at least content.

"Saxon is my best friend. I couldn't take you from him," he explained in a low voice. "If he knew...how I felt, he'd be on his bike and out of here. I know he'd sacrifice his own happiness for mine. I can't let him do that. And not only because of his...sense of direction." He spread his arms out from his sides. "I just couldn't do that to him. I couldn't let him make that sacrifice."

"And yet, you'd sacrifice your *free will*."

"What *difference* would it make?"

"I don't know," she argued. "What...what if I didn't love you anymore?"

His eyes widened with surprise. "*What*?"

"What if I didn't love the new Danjer? The Danjer with no free will. The content Danjer who loved me without passion or jealousy, who fawned over me, who worshipped me. Who never disagreed with me or demanded anything in return. Who was never impatient or cynical or angry. Who had no rough edges.

"Danjer..." she whispered softly, trailing her hand down the dark skin that stretched over his corded biceps. "Danjer, if you only knew. If you only knew how many times I've longed for a quiet, silent, private moment with you. How I've longed for *us*. Not that I don't love Saxon, because I *do*. But sometimes I just wish…to be with you. To wake beside you and watch you in the pale dawn, waiting for the morning sun to spill into the room in a bright wash of light. Watch it on your face before you wake, to watch you turn to me as you open your eyes, to share whispered words, secrets, private thoughts. The kind of things that can't be shared when there are…others.

"I love Saxon," she said. "But I love you just as much. I love you despite the raw violence in your nature…or perhaps because of it. Isn't it enough…to know I feel that way?"

Although he still frowned, some measure of peace entered Danjer's expression as he reached out to push aside the curtain of hair that screened her eyes. "I guess it will have to be," he said softly.

* * * * *

On the other side of the closed bedroom door, Saxon let out a held breath as his shoulders slumped and he leaned against the wall. As he squeezed his eyes tightly shut, his heart was a heavy lump of slag weighing in his chest.

There were some things a man was better off not knowing. And he'd have given *anything*…not to have known how Danjer and Pink felt about each other. He knew Danjer was in love. And he knew that it was a first for the Earther. But, despite Danjer's passion for Pink and despite his aggressively possessive nature, Saxon had somehow hoped to fit himself into the equation.

Because he was in love, too.

His shoulders slumped a little lower as a low sigh hissed between his teeth. Danjer was never going to be happy as long as he had to share Pink's love.

And despite Pink's claim to love both men, Saxon had always felt there was something special going on between Danjer and Pink. He was certain Pink would never love him with the same kind of electric passion she reserved for his best friend.

Silently, he cursed himself and the question that had brought him upstairs. If only his brain were mended, he'd never have climbed the stairs to ask about the word that had slipped his mind. With his lips pressed together in determination, he turned and took a step away from the door before he halted again.

Danjer would just follow, he realized. Danjer would follow him if he were to leave.

Turning back to face the door, he stared at it for several long seconds. Finally clenching his fists and throwing back his shoulders, he pasted a determined smile on his face and pushed through the door. A sharp crack followed by a dull boom announced the first cruel electrical lashings of the evening's storm.

He found them together, Danjer cupping Pink's chin, holding her face as his lips pulled long, liquid kisses out of her mouth along with soft murmurs from her throat. Loudly, Saxon laughed and they jumped apart, Pink's expression guilty while Danjer's was defensive.

Six long determined strides took him across the room where he fisted a hand in Danjer's jersey wrap, yanked him forward a foot, drew back his other fist and threw it at Danjer's face. Twin forks of lighting flashed behind the tinted window and there was a dull thud of splitting skin along with Pink's scream of disbelief. Danjer staggered backward in Saxon's grasp, but Saxon kept a firm grip on the jersey wrap clenched tightly in the mallet of his hand.

Saxon laughed. "Sacrifice? You thought I would sacrifice myself for *you*? *For this*? *For her*?" he spat. "You thought I would sacrifice myself for a faithless friend and this cold-hearted little…little…" His throat closed and he almost choked on the cruel word that he couldn't make come forth.

Danjer wiped his bloodied mouth with the back of one hand, glaring daggers back at Saxon. "*Don't!*" Danjer shouted. "*Don't* say something I won't be able to forgive you for. Don't you dare say a word against her, Saxon!"

"Don't worry, Danjer. I wouldn't waste a word on either of you! Unless maybe it was goodbye," he grated.

"I know what you're thinking, Saxon. But you *can't* leave her," Danjer argued immediately. "She needs you as much as she needs me."

"She needs me like she needs your middle finger," Saxon spat back. "I suggest you use it to complete the circuit. Either that or use the dull end of a crossbow bolt. That ought to work! I'll send you the thickest one I can find."

"That's not what I'm talking about, Saxon," Danjer rushed to argue. "I'm talking about everything else. I'm talking about what happened this afternoon and…what almost happened. She needs you, Saxon," he insisted. "I need you," he added hoarsely.

But Saxon laughed in his face.

"I *know* what you're doing, Saxon," Danjer warned, his voice desperate. "I won't let you sacrifice yourself for me."

Saxon laughed again as he tightened his hold on the front of Danjer's wrap. "No, you don't," he rasped. "You have no idea what I'm doing. Here's your sacrifice," Saxon snarled, pulling his elbow back a second time, then hesitating fractionally when he realized Danjer wasn't going to fight back or even shield himself. Gritting his teeth until he thought his jaw would break, Saxon set his mouth. Pink was hanging from his fighting arm, screaming his name, as he threw his fist again—as hard as he could. Danjer's head snapped backward and his lights went out as he sagged in Saxon's grip.

Outside, the sky rumbled and growled in angry discontent. Saxon held Danjer's unconscious body as it slumped toward the floor. Gently, Saxon eased him downward to sprawl on the tiles, two fingers on the pulse at his neck. For a grim moment, he stared at Pink, now on her knees beside the unconscious man, gathering Danjer's dark head into her lap. He opened his mouth in an attempt to force out something nasty, but only pressed his lips together again, unable to bring himself to the act. He shook his head. "Goodbye, Pink," he croaked, then turned his face from her quickly as he strode across the room and out the door. There was a spatter and slash of sound as the storm's first driving drops of rain were hurled against the windows.

Horrified, Pink stared at the empty doorway. Then she started slapping Danjer's face. "Wake up, wake up, wake up," she moaned. "Oh please, Danjer. Wake up!" Jumping to her feet, she scrambled across the room to snatch up a vase filled with desert floss. Flinging the froth of flowers to the ground, she raced back to Danjer and dashed the sloshing water into his face. Helplessly, she stared at his closed eyes before she sank to her knees and grabbed his wrap at the shoulders. Crying hot, fat tears, she shook him violently and shouted his name. There was a quick succession of flashing light behind her then the accompanying clap of thunder but it didn't hide the hum of the garage doors sliding open.

Danjer opened his eyes with a start. "Saxon," he gasped. Immediately Pink was dragging him to his feet as she pulled him toward the door. Groggily, he shook his head as she tugged at him, her fists bunched in his wrap. Stumbling, he went to his knees.

"Get up, get up, get up!" she pleaded, still yanking on his shirt.

"Pink!" he barked as he pushed her aside and got to his feet. "Stop it!" Then his cleats were skidding on the tiled floor as he propelled himself out of the room and toward the stairs descending two levels to the garage. Saxon's recharge slot was empty and the garage door was closed as Danjer rocketed down the stairs with Pink racing to follow him. He didn't hesitate when he found the axe buried in the display screen of his tracking system. Wrenching the weapon out of his console, he threw it aside.

"Get on," he shouted as he straddled his bike and dropped onto the saddle. Reaching for the console, he flipped several switches—then cursed viciously as he palmed them into the off position and reached lower to reset the breaker on the side of the bike. Pink felt him take a breath and hold it as he flipped the starter again.

"No!" he almost screamed as he shoved back on the saddle and opened the energy compartment...to find the square slotted space empty. "Bastard!" he yelled in perfect fury. "Fucking bastard!" Throwing his leg over the front of his bike, he raced up the stairs again, returning less than a minute later with an assortment of square storage wafers scavenged from various household appliances, none of which would slot into the energy compartment.

"Give me your necklace," he commanded tersely as he dropped to one knee beside the bike. Pulling the copper strands apart with a yank, he separated them with a deft hand and then twisted the copper wires together with the pretty scored squares, slotting the connectors onto the sides of the largest storage wafer.

Noticing her stunned expression, he shot her a hard grin. "Always have a backup plan," he told her. "And always keep your toolkit handy."

She frowned as she watched him work. "That won't be enough," she pointed out swiftly, reaching for a second wafer. "Connect them in series," she instructed him.

Following her directions, he fitted the resultant assembly into the energy compartment. Almost immediately, he pulled it out again to twist and shorten the wires. Holding his breath, he lowered the arrangement into the energy box again, sliding the scored connectors down into the compartment's slotted outlets. "Cross your fingers," he told her.

Nodding, she scooted back on the bike's saddle, leaving room for him to climb on. He flipped a switch and the bike lifted. A voice command opened the garage door and they sped out into the black, lightning-ripped night. Flipping another switch as he exited the garage, a curved antenna grew from the bike's tail and, with the static collector functioning, they blasted out into the gusting rain.

For at least five minutes, Pink remained completely silent so that Danjer could concentrate on Saxon's trail. Vicious, slashing arrows of rain flashed in the weaving beam of the bike's headlight. With the bike's storm navigation system on, the bike dodged and swerved to avoid buildups of electrical energy. Danjer made a sudden left. Finally, Pink could stand the silence no longer. Brimming with anxiety, she dared a question. "Can you see his trail?"

Eyes on the ground, Danjer nodded without speaking.

"Where's he going?"

"Nowhere," Danjer threw over his shoulder. "Straight to nowhere."

"What do you mean, straight to nowhere?"

"He doesn't have his storm navigation system on. He's traveling in straight lines."

"But—he'll be killed!" she cried out hoarsely, her voice still ravaged from her earlier tears.

Danjer nodded and kicked up the speed.

"What is it that you *see*?" she asked after several more quiet moments.

"Bugs," he told her.

"Bugs?"

"Bugs," he repeated, slowing his bike slightly as he scanned the ground. "Sand bugs. When the bikes pass over the ground, the magnetic field changes. The bugs don't know up from down. They pour out of the ground and stagger about like drunks for a while before they can reorient themselves.

Half of them die before they can get back under the ground, either in the hot sun or the cold night or the wet storm. I follow the dead bugs."

"But…how on eYona can you *see* them?" she demanded, staring at the ground and seeing nothing. "They're tiny! No bigger than the smallest pebbles!"

Danjer nodded in agreement. "They're green," he said.

"Green? What's green?"

"It's a color," Danjer told her.

Pink shook her head in confusion. "What's color?"

"Earthers can see colors," Danjer explained briefly. "eYonans can't. That's why I'm a better tracker than Saxon…and every other eYonan on the face of the planet." He shook his head. "I see things differently than you. The sand bugs are bright, fluorescent, brilliant green. They stand out as if they were…incredibly light or densely dark. It's like…following a beam of light. The color fades with time, of course. But that just helps me distinguish one trail from another, an earlier trail from a later one."

"Don't they…blow away?"

He shrugged. "Eventually. But if the trail is fresh, I only need a few to follow."

With this comforting assurance from Danjer, Pink put her cheek against his broad back and tightened her hold around his waist. The wind and rain slashed down, pelting her shoulders and legs, smacking at Danjer's leathers as she stared into the darkness. "How many colors are there?"

"Thousands," he answered. "Three primary colors, three more secondary. Thousands of variations."

"What…color am I?" she asked him.

He reached back to clasp her leg. "You're mostly pink," he told her as he gave her thigh a rough squeeze, "Just like the diamond you wear in your belly. Your hair is the bright color of sunshine and your eyes are green, the color of the forest."

"I thought sunshine was just white," she ventured. "Your eyes," she stammered, "must be the color of…fire, then?"

He shook his head. "More like the color of the sky or the sea."

She shook her head against his broad back. "That's not possible," she insisted. "Your eyes…burn." The bike swerved just then as a jagged bolt of lightning slammed into the ground behind them.

"What color is lightning?" she asked.

"Mostly white," he replied. "And blue around the edges."

"What color are your eyes?" she asked next.

"Blue," he answered.

With this response she nodded her head, finally satisfied.

* * * * *

"Danjer!" Pink suddenly screamed. But he'd already seen it—a bike lying on its side and a crumpled form darkening the ground thirty feet distant. Guiding his bike to the right, Danjer's headlight illuminated Saxon's large leather-clad body awkwardly piled into the ground. In the headlight's beam, Saxon's golden mane was mixed with a cruel thorny crown of black blood. Lightning flashed and the blood was red for a brief, hard instant.

Pink was off the bike and running over the wet sand toward Saxon as Danjer followed through the nightmare-strobed darkness.

"Please," he prayed in a whisper as he moved forward, dragging his leaden feet, wanting to get to Saxon but fearing what he might find. "Please don't let him be dead." Nearby, the black night was split with twin forks of blue-edged lightning.

Swallowing hard, Danjer forced his legs to carry him to Saxon. In that instant, he knew that there was at least one other thing he wanted as much as Pink's love — and that was Saxon's life.

His stomach churned in ugly knots as he traveled between stark flashes of painful memory and lightning-harsh images of threatening reality.

Saxon lying on the ground as blood welled up through the jagged cut in his helm. His face gray. His eyes closed.

Saxon lying on the ground, his head in Pink's lap. A deep split in his scalp at the hairline. His blood dark and red on a tangled gold background. His face white. His eyes green as they opened and he frowned up at Danjer.

"Saxon," Danjer croaked, pulling him up in one mighty heave and wrapping him in an utterly male embrace of love. "Jeezis Skies," he growled in a breaking voice, "I love you, Saxon."

Saxon pulled away from him with a curious grin. "Aw," he drawled, "I bet you say that to all the guys."

Squinting hard in the pelting rain, Danjer laughed, weak with relief as he yelled at his friend, "Are you okay? How do you feel?"

Very slowly, very carefully, Saxon moved his head from side to side. "Like I was hit by lightning."

Danjer nodded with a grin as Saxon looked carefully to the left.

"What are we doing here?"

"What do you mean — here?"

"I mean, what are we doing here, south of Aranthea," Saxon asked, pointing north, "when the last thing I remember was fighting beside you at D'Almiers?"

"D'Almiers! D'Almiers was a year ago!"

Saxon tilted his head, eyes narrowed quizzically as he grinned. "Did I miss much?"

"Yeah!" Danjer laughed with pure, real pleasure. "Yeah, you did!"

"So fill me in," he said easily, striding carefully toward his bike and turning the machine upright.

"Well, to begin with, you got hit in the head at D'Almiers and...and...how's your sense of direction?" Danjer asked sharply.

Saxon shrugged. "As good as ever, I reckon."

"Which way's south, then?"

Saxon looked at him like he was mad then slowly turned around to face southward. But he stopped when he found Pink standing just behind him. Her short wet hair was plastered against her face and she was crying...but she was still beautiful. For several instants Saxon just stared, tilting his head slowly. Then he returned his gaze to Danjer.

"Who's that?" he asked, dividing his attention between Danjer and the imp. "She's—"

"Beautiful," Danjer finished for him without thinking.

"I don't need you to tell me that, you backworld barbarian!"

"Sorry," Danjer apologized. "I didn't mean to put words in your mouth." He shrugged. "It's an old habit."

"Tell me something useful," Saxon admonished. "*Tell* me she's my girlfriend," he implored as he scanned his friend's gaze.

Pink stood in the slashing rain, her small fists doubled into tight, white knots at her sides. And Danjer understood exactly what she was going through. He knew she needed to touch Saxon, to reassure herself that he was really alive—as Danjer himself had just done. She needed to feel his body warm against her own, needed to press her ear against his chest and hear for herself the giant heartbeat that drummed within his rib cage.

Still, she held back as she stared hungrily at the two men. She held back, waiting for Danjer's answer.

"As if you could get that lucky," Danjer snorted after a moment's hesitation. He shook his head regretfully but his eyes were lit with mischief. "She's not *your* girlfriend, you great, ignorant outlander." Danjer reached out and pulled Pink between them. Taking Pink's arms, he wrapped them around Saxon's waist then snugged himself up against her backside. "She's our girlfriend," he told his best friend.

"Really?" Saxon tilted one eyebrow upward as he wiped his brow with the back of his hand. "How did that come about?"

Danjer shrugged. "She didn't want to break up a team."

Saxon licked his bottom lip as he gazed down at Pink's head, pressed against his chest. "Do you...think there's any chance she'll let me tie her down?"

Danjer nodded. "That's not a problem. But she *is* a bit particular about where you kiss her. And you might as well know, we're marrying her."

"Don't I get any say in the matter?" Saxon argued with a pleased smile.

"Jeezis Skies, Saxon. You're my best friend. I wouldn't leave you out of this. *You* get to say 'I do'."

"And what do I get to say?" Pink asked with a shaky laugh as she clung to Saxon and turned her gaze on Danjer.

The rain lightened to a gentle patter as the three lovers stood entwined.

"You?" Danjer murmured warmly against her hair. "You get to tell us how much you love us...for the rest of our lives."

Why an electronic book?

We live in the Information Age — an exciting time in the history of human civilization, in which technology rules supreme and continues to progress in leaps and bounds every minute of every day. For a multitude of reasons, more and more avid literary fans are opting to purchase e-books instead of paper books. The question from those not yet initiated into the world of electronic reading is simply: *Why?*

1. ***Price.*** An electronic title at Ellora's Cave Publishing and Cerridwen Press runs anywhere from 40% to 75% less than the cover price of the exact same title in paperback format. Why? Basic mathematics and cost. It is less expensive to publish an e-book (no paper and printing, no warehousing and shipping) than it is to publish a paperback, so the savings are passed along to the consumer.

2. ***Space.*** Running out of room in your house for your books? That is one worry you will never have with electronic books. For a low one-time cost, you can purchase a handheld device specifically designed for e-reading. Many e-readers have large, convenient screens for viewing. Better yet, hundreds of titles can be stored within your new library — on a single microchip. There a variety of e-readers from different manufacturers. You can also read e-books on your PC or laptop computer. (Please note that Ellora's Cave does not endorse any specific brands.

You can check our websites at www.ellorascave.com or www.cerridwenpress.com for information we make available to new consumers.)

3. *Mobility.* Because your new e-library consists of only a microchip within a small, easily transportable e-reader, your entire cache of books can be taken with you wherever you go.

4. *Personal Viewing Preferences.* Are the words you are currently reading too small? Too large? Too... ANNOYING? Paperback books cannot be modified according to personal preferences, but e-books can.

5. *Instant Gratification.* Is it the middle of the night and all the bookstores near you are closed? Are you tired of waiting days, sometimes weeks, for bookstores to ship the novels you bought? Ellora's Cave Publishing sells instantaneous downloads twenty-four hours a day, seven days a week, every day of the year. Our webstore is never closed. Our e-book delivery system is 100% automated, meaning your order is filled as soon as you pay for it.

Those are a few of the top reasons why electronic books are replacing paperbacks for many avid readers.

As always, Ellora's Cave and Cerridwen Press welcome your questions and comments. We invite you to email us at Comments@ellorascave.com or write to us directly at Ellora's Cave Publishing Inc., 1056 Home Avenue, Akron, OH 44310-3502.

COMING TO A BOOKSTORE NEAR YOU!

ELLORA'S CAVE

Bestselling Authors Tour

UPDATES AVAILABLE AT

WWW.ELLORASCAVE.COM

Cerridwen, the Celtic Goddess of wisdom, was the muse who brought inspiration to storytellers and those in the creative arts. Cerridwen Press encompasses the best and most innovative stories in all genres of today's fiction. Visit our site and discover the newest titles by talented authors who still get inspired - much like the ancient storytellers did, once upon a time.

Cerridwen Press

www.cerridwenpress.com